# Praise for *Dead Drop*

*"Norton has created an engaging protagonist in Amy, who is bright, brave and tenacious. The tale features a small cast of characters, as many players disappear shortly after being introduced, so Amy has to carry the narrative load. Fortunately, she's up to the challenge; readers should quickly get invested in what happens to the feisty, heady heroine. With a neat twist in her fast-paced narrative, the author illustrates how events from 80 years in the past can affect people in the present, even Amy herself. Norton seamlessly blends history and mystery into a spellbinding thriller. This sequel accomplishes the unlikely feat of making an insurance investigator enthralling."*

~ Kirkus Reviews

## Praise for *Sweet Dreams, Sweet Death*
## Also by P.K. Norton

*"I think you will enjoy this one and as for me – well I'm looking forward to more in this series!"*

~ Miki Hope

*"An impressively crafted and unfailingly entertaining novel by a master of the genre,* Sweet Dreams, Sweet Death *by P.K. Norton is the first volume of what promises to be a simply outstanding new series starring Amy Lynch, female investigator."*

~James A. Cox
Editor-in-Chief, Midwest Book Review

*"A fine debut novel by an up-and-coming writer. I look forward t more Amy Lynch stories!..."*

~Amazon customer

*"This is the sort of book you can curl up with for an evening and enjoy. While typically I suppose murder wouldn't be considered a light topic. P.K. Norton provides you with an easy read that will keep you guessing until the big reveal. I would definitely recommend this for murder mystery lovers as well as for those who like a bit of intrigue in their romance."*

~@kleffnotes

# DEAD DROP

## An Amy Lynch Investigation

P.K. NORTON

Visit our website at www.StillwaterPress.com for more information.

First Stillwater River Publications Edition

ISBN-13: 978-1-946-30048-5
ISBN-10: 1-946-30048-9

1 2 3 4 5 6 7 8 9 10
Written by P.K. Norton
Published by Stillwater River Publications, Glocester, RI, USA.

# Dedication

As always, for Jack, my partner in life and in crime.

# Acknowledgements

With heartfelt thanks to everyone who encourages and supports me in my writing. Special thanks to the members of my critique groups: Ruth, Katherine, Toby, Barry, Debi and Pam. Also thanks to Jane and Lindsy for their editing skills and suggestions. And, of course, thanks to Jack for getting me started on this journey.

# Chapter 1

# Judas - Paris 1943

*Don't panic. You must not panic.* He had trouble following his own advice as he hurried down the darkened street. The sound of footsteps behind him grew louder, more insistent, matching the frantic beating of his heart, replacing the din of the anti-aircraft guns as the bombers flew eastward. The echo of footfalls indicated at least two people.

*Steady. Keep moving. Stay calm. You can lose them. You must.* He held his breath, trying to judge their distance from him. They were gaining ground. His so-called comrades from the Résistance were nearly upon him.

They knew of his betrayal. And he knew what they'd do if they caught him. They'd brand him a traitor, a Judas. It wouldn't be like with Antoine, a single bullet to the head. No, his own death would be long and cruel. They'd torture him until they learned everything he knew, everything he'd done—the names, the plans. Only then would they kill him.

*Just a couple more blocks to reach safety. Make the darkness work for you. You're almost there. Stay calm. Don't run. You'll be safe soon.*

At last he reached the rue Jean Jaurès and the designated spot—an ordinary house, one amid a row of ordinary houses in a middle-class neighborhood of St. Denis. Without stopping, he opened his fist and shoved the crumpled envelope into a meter-high cement urn next to a low stone wall, then continued down the street, ever aware of his pursuers.

At the corner, a crowd emerged from a theater. He eased himself into their midst and disappeared into the darkness. *I'll be all right now. Help will come. They'll get me out. Like they promised. They'll help me escape to somewhere far away and safe. And I'll be rich. Rich beyond belief.*

A sudden blast sent him reeling. Heart pounding, he found shelter in a doorway. His pursuers stumbled past, looking for him in the confusion. He looked around. A single plane, trailing fire, was flying to the west, having jettisoned a load of bombs not far from where he stood. They'd hit the very spot that had held his hopes for rescue, for survival. Judas slumped away into the darkness, unsure of how to save himself.

# Chapter 2

# Paris 2003

My second day in France, I got lost in St. Denis. Not a good place to do so. This sketchy suburb north of Paris had a population that was heavily immigrant, usually communist and often unemployed. The crime rate was uncomfortably high.

I probably shouldn't have been there alone; that was never the plan. My boyfriend Pete was supposed to be with me, spending a glorious month in Paris, volunteering with me at an archaeological dig. But at the last minute, a case of his was scheduled for trial weeks earlier than expected. So here I was, feeling a tiny bit vulnerable on my first solo trip, and beginning to question my own judgment. Still, I was determined not to spend my time looking over my shoulder like a wimp.

Many people go to France to see Paris. They visit the Eiffel Tower, the Arc de Triomphe, the Champs Elysées. Not me. On a sunny Sunday afternoon in August, I was searching the streets of St. Denis for the archaeological site where I'd be working. So far, all I'd found were cookie-cutter high-rise apartment buildings and dark, narrow old streets lined with trash and decaying tenements. I was not encouraged.

Arriving at what I hoped was the rue de Strasbourg—but with no identifying signage—I came upon a corrugated aluminum fence, about seven feet high, lining both sides of the street—just the sort of structure one might use to cordon off an urban dig. Finding a narrow opening, I peeked into the gap for a closer look.

Before my eyes could register anything noteworthy, a voice behind me demanded "*Qu-est-ce que vous faites là?* / What are you doing there?"

I gasped and reached for the pepper spray in my pocket. If this man intended to mug me, I was damned if I'd make it easy for him. No way would I be a helpless victim. Spinning around, I faced my potential assailant.

He raised his hands in surrender. "*Ne tirez pas* / Don't shoot. I am unarmed." He was of average height, with brown hair and brown eyes, probably in his early forties. He flashed me an impish grin.

I relaxed my grip on the pepper spray, but backed away a few feet—in case he knew karate. Pulling myself up to my full four feet eleven inches, I looked him square in the face. "I start working on this dig tomorrow and wanted to get a look at the site today. A little advance reconnaissance," I told him in my rusty Canadian French.

"*Ah, je vois.* / I see. In that case, I bid you welcome." His grin expanded into a big, toothy smile. "I am Michel Toussaint. It is a pleasure to meet you, *Mademoiselle*…?"

*Oh shit! The head of the dig. So much for making a good first impression.* I looked down at my cut-off jeans and Star Trek T-shirt, willing myself not to blush. "I'm Amy Lynch, volunteer digger for the month of August. You haven't exactly caught me at my best."

"*Ah, oui*, the American volunteer. We are happy you will be working with us. But where is your friend Peter, our other volunteer?"

"I'm sorry to say he won't be able to join us."

"A pity. Nevertheless, I am most happy to welcome you." Smile lines circled his eyes. "Advance reconnaissance, eh?" he chuckled as he unlocked a gate in the aluminum fence. "In that case, *ma chère Mademoiselle*, please allow me to show you our work in progress." He bowed and made a sweeping gesture to usher me into the area.

I took a few steps forward.

"Tread carefully," he warned. "We have two areas of significant depth here. It can be dangerous."

I ventured inside.

"Here we have three separate digging operations, or cuttings: the gravesite, the habitation and the pit." He pointed to each.

The gravesite was a shallow area marked off with string and draped in heavy plastic, protecting it from the elements. Large mounds of dirt flanked the sides. The habitation was a hole in the ground about seven or eight feet deep with walls of light-colored stone blocks cut into regular sized squares. The final section was a rectangular pit about fifteen feet wide by twenty feet long and at least twenty feet deep. A thick wooden beam nearly two feet wide spanned this crater from front to back. I peeked down to see several large piles of soil.

"These areas look fascinating, M. Toussaint. Working on a dig has been a dream of mine for years. I have so many questions I'm not sure where to begin. Please, tell me everything." I was sucking up big time, but I meant it sincerely.

Toussaint beamed, surveyed the area with his eyes, then began, "*S'il vous plaît* / please call me Michel. This is a salvage dig, made possible because of planned urban renewal. When an existing building is knocked down, or otherwise destroyed, the government ministry allows us to investigate the site before new construction begins. We are happy for such a valuable opportunity. Sadly, the time allowed is always too short."

"What have you found so far?"

"The city of St. Denis dates back many centuries. Most of what we have unearthed to date is of medieval origin. The site is even older than that. We found some evidence of habitation dating back to the eighth century."

Toussaint waved his arm toward the area covered in clear plastic. "Here you see a burial ground. The human skeletons are beginning to take shape. We take special pains with them, as they are most fragile. Also, it is critical to treat these bones with the utmost respect. Failure to do so would be a sacrilege, a desecration. We have no wish to insult the dead."

"Weren't these people buried in coffins?" I asked.

"Excellent question, *mon amie*. We have found some metal handles and a few nails, most likely from coffins. The coffins themselves would not have withstood the ravages of time. Wood decomposes. Bones are more durable."

"How old are the bodies?"

"Probably sixteenth century, judging from the depth of the graves and the nature and quality of the materials recovered. To the right, you can see the traces of a habitation dating back to around the twelfth century. The artifacts have been removed and the area cleaned. We are now beginning to examine the remains of the structure."

I studied the area in question while waiting for him to continue.

"Finally, over here, you see the most ancient of the areas at this site, from the seventh century. This site contained items of considerable interest—buttons and needles fashioned from bones, *par example*."

"What are those piles of dirt down there?"

"Since this area had told us everything it could, we now use this pit as a repository for soil removed from the gravesite and the habitation, *naturellement* after sifting it to recover all artifacts, however small."

He hesitated. "Would you like to see more? I can show you another site in the early stages of investigation."

"Yes, please."

He led me into the street with a spring in his step. I wished I could be that enthused about my job investigating insurance claims back in Boston. Had that been the case, I wouldn't be taking a full month's vacation in the middle of the summer despite the strong protests of my bully of a boss. He had a way of making life difficult.

"Here we are," Toussaint said as we approached a site at the other end of the street. He removed a key chain from his pocket and unlocked the gate. "This is the area which fascinates me most at present."

"Is this section very old?"

"Not at all. It dates from World War II."

"World War II? That's recent history, not archaeology. Can't you learn as much from newspaper archives as you could from this site?"

"*Ah, non, mon amie,* you are mistaken." Toussaint's voice became hushed, his face solemn. "Much history from that time has never been recorded, yet it is of great interest. Secrets from the recent past are secrets nonetheless. One never knows where they may lead." He stopped speaking, his eyes focused on some distant spot.

The man remained motionless, staring, for what felt like several minutes.

Shifting my weight from one foot to the other, I wondered if he had forgotten I was there. I cleared my throat in a most unladylike manner. "That sounds mysterious. What exactly have you found?" I looked around at an assortment of large stones, or small boulders, scattered on the ground, intermixed with pieces of rotting lumber. Nothing remotely resembling the orderliness of the other site.

He blinked a few times and turned his gaze in my direction. Gone was the warm, charming man who had been giving me a tour. His replacement appeared more businesslike, with a stiff, cold demeanor, rather like an unfriendly college professor.

"The ruins you see here are what remain of a bombed-out building. We have learned from newspaper accounts that a crippled English bomber jettisoned its load in this vicinity. One of the bombs detonated. The safety mechanisms in place to prevent such an occurrence apparently failed. What malfunctioned to cause this disaster, we may never learn. We have just completed demolition of the building and begun to clean and document the area." Toussaint screwed up his face and shuddered ever so slightly.

I scrutinized the scene. What in the world could he find so interesting in this mess? And what was that odd look on his face? "You haven't told me what you've found here."

Toussaint's eyes clouded over as he frowned at me. "Your curiosity will serve you well in life, *Mademoiselle*. For the moment, though, I must decline to answer your question. At least until more is known. It may prove to be nothing, but until that has been determined, I prefer to remain silent."

Why did he bring me to this site if he didn't want to talk about it? And where had his friendly smile gone? "No problem. Which area will I be working on tomorrow?"

"Tomorrow? *Sacré bleu!* I shall be absent from the site for the next two days. Unavoidable business." His smile returned. "I am pleased to have made your acquaintance today."

"Shall I report to someone else?"

Toussaint bit his lower lip. "I apologize for my lack of thought. Of course you need to know what to do. Marie Duprès, one of our senior archaeologists, will be expecting you. She is responsible for operations in my absence."

"Where will I find her?"

"In the office, at 8 rue de Strasbourg. Three blocks from here, and to the left. The building is easy to locate, well-marked, unlike the areas you have seen today." He headed to the gate as he spoke.

"What time shall I report?"

"Our day begins at 9:00. You may wish to arrive a few minutes early." He hurried into the street. "I must say good-bye now. A colleague is expecting me. I must not be late. Until Wednesday, then." He locked the gate, glanced at his watch and dashed down the street.

I stood alone wondering what the hell caused the abrupt change in Toussaint, and frustrated that I'd have to wait until the next day to learn more. Two things I knew already: Michel Toussaint was an intriguing man, though with something slightly off about him, and working with him couldn't help but be interesting. Tomorrow morning couldn't come soon enough.

# Chapter 3

The next day, I arrived in St. Denis earlier than necessary, despite my body still being on Boston time and somewhat sleep-deprived. With nearly an hour to spare, I took the long route to the office, by way of the two dig sites Michel Toussaint had shown me. Along the way I watched the municipal workers in green coveralls washing down the sidewalks with water flowing from the gutters. No wonder the city looked so clean.

A crowd was gathered at the entrance to the older work area, a very noisy crowd. I moved closer to see what was happening.

"*Mais non, Mademoiselle. C'est interdit.* / I'm sorry ma'am. You can't go in there." A policeman blocked my way.

"It's OK. I work here." Not exactly a lie. I stood there a few moments, waiting for the man to become distracted. When he looked away, I wormed my way in through the crowd. Being short is sometimes an advantage.

In no time, I regretted my action. Unprepared for the sight that greeted me at the edge of the largest pit, I backed away and closed my eyes—to no avail. When I opened them, the body was still there, lying at the bottom of the pit, the head at an impossible angle. From where I stood, there was no doubt. Michel Toussaint was dead.

I forced my gaze to linger where the body lay—not easy for me, but important. The last time I had seen a dead body in situ, it was my fiancé Danny, lying in a ditch where his car had run off the road. That was three years ago. I'll never get over it, but I stopped crying in public ages ago. Right now, I needed to assure the inner Amy that Danny wasn't down there. The body was that of a man I had met only yesterday.

What had happened? I studied the people on the sidewalk, looking for someone who might have answers. They came in all ages, sizes and shapes. Many were dressed like me—cut-off jeans, T-shirts and sneakers. Others looked like neighborhood residents, dressed in faded work clothes, a few with more children than teeth. Many of them were exchanging angry words with the police, who held their ground, refusing to allow anyone to approach the pit and trying to eject everyone who was already there. Nobody appeared to be in charge. Nobody acknowledged my presence.

So much for my vacation plans. The company I worked for—New England Casualty and Indemnity—was insuring this dig. That was how I learned of the work and came to volunteer here. Now, as an experienced claims investigator, and the only NEC&I employee on-site, I needed to get to work. I stood silently, deciding what to do.

My immediate priority was to report to Marie Duprès. Toussaint had said she was his second-in-command. I approached a tall young man with sandy hair and a Slavic look. "Excuse me. I'm looking for Marie Duprès. Do you know where she is?"

"*Pardon*? Marie Duprès?" He flashed me a crooked smile. "I am sorry. I do not know." He turned away.

I opted to stay put for a bit and listen to what people had to say. The crowd was getting larger and more vociferous by the minute. My brain needed to adjust to hearing French again, and Parisian French at that, not the Québécois version I was accustomed to.

I spotted an attractive young man with light hair and hazel eyes. He was short, slender—at maybe five foot three—downright petite. Just my size. I almost hugged him.

"*Bonjour*. My name's Amy Lynch. I'm looking for Marie Duprès."

"*Ah, oui*. The American volunteer. In all the confusion this morning, your impending arrival slipped my mind. I am André Savard." He bowed and shook my hand. Was he going to click his heels as well?

"Marie was here a few moments ago, doing her best to deal with this terrible tragedy. She and Michel were close friends." His voice shook as he spoke. His face clouded over. "I fear there will be no work today."

"Yes," I said. "It's horrible. Do you know what happened?"

He hesitated a moment, visibly working at composing himself. "About fifteen minutes ago, we arrived for work—myself, Pierre and Georges. The gate to the more ancient site was unlocked. We assumed Marie had arrived early to inspect something. We remained unconcerned, expecting to see her, but instead found Michel, who was supposed to be absent today, lying on the foundation of the deepest work area. The only ladder long enough to reach the bottom was on the far side of the pit. We couldn't get down to him." He let out a ragged breath.

I could see what he meant. The pit was edged on two sides by a corrugated aluminum fence, with no room to walk. The wooden beam which yesterday had spanned the area from front to back now lay at the bottom. There was no way to reach the ladder on the opposite side.

I shuddered. "What did you do?"

"We telephoned for help. The local police arrived almost immediately. We now await the arrival of the ambulance and, *hélas*, the medical examiner. *Ah, voilà Pierre. Excusez-moi*, Amy." André Savard hurried off.

I looked around, trying to zero in on the commotion around me. Some people stared into the pit, their eyes glazed over. Others averted their gaze. The noise was chaotic, in French, German, and another language I couldn't begin to identify. A young woman with short red curls wailed loudly.

"But this is crazy. Why do we have to wait here? Somebody needs to take charge." The speaker, an older, red-faced man in khaki pants and a faded green shirt forced his way toward the pit, only to be blocked by the policemen.

"*Mais non, Monsieur*," one of the policemen said. "We cannot have you people walking about in here, disturbing the accident scene."

"What about you people disturbing our dig site?" the man replied. "Possibly destroying valuable artifacts and irreplaceable information. Isn't that important as well?"

"How did anybody get into this site anyway?" a young woman wanted to know. She had straight black hair cascading down her back, and long skinny legs, and wore white short-shorts and a polka-dot halter top.

"I don't know," the older man replied. "The lock isn't broken. It makes no sense at all." He appeared on the verge of tears. "And the other work area—my site—is ruined as well. It will be impossible to determine the damage that has been caused. Years of history destroyed. My studies may never recover from this."

"What happened at your site, Claude?" asked a tall young man. He wore cut-off jeans and a T-shirt that said "University of Massachusetts." Fluent French, lovely accent, a certain *je ne sais quoi* about him. Definitely not from UMass.

"My site has been ransacked," Claude announced. "We had just dismantled the remains of the structure and cleaned the surface in preparation for the more intensive work. Now whatever was there is lost for all time. Such a senseless crime. And someone broke into my office as well. The place is in complete disorder. Such an outrage."

"Never mind your precious site or your damn office, Claude," said a voice from somewhere in the crowd. "A man is dead here. A good man. A brilliant scientist. That is the real tragedy."

The people in the crowd roared, echoing this sentiment.

The unseen voice continued, "Besides, with the mess in your office, I don't know how you could tell if anything had been disturbed anyway."

I escaped into the street to collect my thoughts. The morning air was still cool. The quiet sounded wonderful. In the end, there wasn't much to think about: Michel Toussaint was dead. The worksite was closed, at least for the moment. And I needed to begin an investigation. Fast.

# Chapter 4

Walking toward the World War II site, I reviewed the possibilities surrounding Toussaint's death. Had he jumped? Had he fallen? Had he been pushed? The answer would be critical in settling a claim. An accidental death would be covered; a suicide maybe not. The policy would cover vandalism damage to the office but probably not to either dig site. Coverage for work in progress would be too complicated for any company except Lloyd's of London. If Lloyd's was underwriting that particular work-site exposure, Toussaint's death might be their bailiwick as well.

How cold that sounded. How selfish. A man I knew, albeit briefly, was dead and here I was looking for a loophole for my company. Not a good feeling. My non-professional self was much nicer.

The World War II site was locked. I peered through an opening in the gate. The area was still a semi-organized pile of rubble. I stood at the gate and stared—to no avail. I had only glanced at this area on my tour with Toussaint yesterday; I saw no difference today.

I needed to seek out that man, Claude, who had been so upset about this site. He should know what had been disturbed and, hopefully, if anything had been taken. What could there possibly have been to steal?

I also wanted to examine Toussaint's records of the work on both sites. If he was as good as his reputation, he would have made complete records of the area during each phase of the project—photographs, diagrams, the works. At least that was what my old archaeology professor would have done. It was a place to start. I needed photos of the site in its present condition. Fast. Unfortunately, my camera was back at the *pension* where I was staying. Not much use to me there. After all, I had come here today to dig, not to investigate. If only I had had the foresight to buy one of those new cell phones with the built-in camera.

With nothing more to learn here at the moment, I headed back to where Toussaint's body lay. An ambulance was just outside the entrance to the worksite, as well as three other vehicles, all illegally parked. Each car had a dashboard placard which read: *Presse*.

The reporters were easy to spot, each accompanied by a photographer. They were milling around the entrance to the site, trying to convince the guard to allow them in.

The police ignored the media people. The diggers remained at the gate, staring at the potential intruders, defying them to come any closer.

André Savard approached me just outside the gate. "I apologize for my lack of courtesy earlier. The manner in which I deserted you was quite rude. Please allow me to make up for that. It must be difficult for you to encounter this tragedy on your first day."

"I'll be fine, André, but thank you. Will the dig be closed during the investigation?"

"Perhaps, perhaps not. We shall resume our work as soon as the authorities allow. A new head archaeologist must be named. Most likely Marie Duprès will be chosen. Have you located her yet?"

"No, but I need to speak with her soon." *And discuss filing a claim.* André didn't need to know that. Not yet.

The police grouped together for a conference, trying to figure out how to get down into the pit to examine the body.

André and I used this opportunity to slip into the site and approach the pit. Nobody registered our presence as two uniformed officers hurried off. The remaining policemen focused on the area at the side of the pit where the beam had been anchored. There was now a gaping hole surrounded by eroded dirt and stone. An officer said, "Apparently the beam came loose from its supports as Toussaint was crossing over yesterday."

I turned to André. "That can't be."

"Why not?" The officer cocked his head in my direction. "And how did you get in here?"

I chose to answer his first question. "It can't be so because I saw Michel Toussaint here yesterday. I spoke with him. He showed me both worksites. The beam was in place, and intact. That was in the afternoon."

"I see. He must have returned later."

"On a Sunday evening?"

"*Oui. Pourquoi pas*? /Why not?" André said. If he thought of something he wished to examine? When a brilliant man of science has a question, or an idea, he wishes to investigate at once. Do you not agree, Amy?"

"You could be right." I pondered Toussaint's sudden departure yesterday and his erratic behavior. He had told me he'd be away for a few days, returning to the dig on Wednesday. He could have come back sooner, but it struck me as odd. Also, Toussaint was an educated, experienced archaeologist, not a fool. He wouldn't have allowed an unsafe beam to be used for crossing the pit. He would have ensured that the side braces were adequate.

I was about to explain all this to André when the police approached. *Be nice, I warned myself. You'll need a copy of their report for your file.*

One of the men in street clothes—a detective, I guessed—addressed us. "*Excusez-moi*. Do you have business here?"

André said, "I discovered the body. I work at the dig. And this is Amy Lynch, a volunteer who has recently joined us."

"I have some questions for you." The detective motioned to André with his hand. "*Par ici, s'il vous plaît*. / This way please." He removed a pencil and small notebook from his breast pocket and led André out of my ear-shot. Another policeman was questioning the fellow with the U Mass T-shirt.

"And you, *Mademoiselle*, we have questions for you as well."

I turned to see a third man frowning at me.

The frown couldn't hide the fact that this guy was totally adorable. Medium height, fit without being muscle-bound, with brown eyes and curly brown hair. He was carrying a black leather handbag—nothing feminine, more of a man purse. I hoped I could make him smile. Odds were he had at least one dimple. Not that I was in the market for romance. Things were going great back home with my boyfriend Pete. Besides, I was here to work. Didn't hurt to look, though.

"I am *Inspecteur* Paul Béchard," the detective announced, "from the *Préfecture de Police* in Paris."

"Paris? But we're in St. Denis. Isn't this a separate city, a different jurisdiction?" I needed to learn when to shut up. No point challenging the man. It was a great way to get myself into trouble, international style.

"*Mais oui* / that is so. I find myself assigned to St. Denis every August when the local office is under-staffed due to vacations." He wrinkled his brow. "Now, if you have no objections, I will be the one who asks the questions." He flipped to a new page in his notebook and cast a stern look in my direction. "Your name again, please?"

"Amy Lynch." I spelled it.

"Nationality?"

"American."

"I would have thought you were Canadian."

"That's understandable. I lived in Québec for a few years. Picked up my accent there."

"May I see your identification?"

I gulped. "Sorry. I don't have my papers with me. I came here this morning expecting to work on the dig. My passport and visa are at the *pension* where I'm staying."

"I see. You are aware of the importance of carrying your papers at all times when in a foreign country?" There was that frown again.

"I am now. Sorry."

"*Eh bien*, Mademoiselle Lynch, tell me why you are at the site of a police investigation. I left specific instructions with the local officers that no employees were allowed access until our work is completed."

"I realize that, *Inspecteur*. I apologize if I have caused any problem, but I need to investigate some things as well."

"*Comment*? / What do you mean?" His frown deepened.

"I work for the company that insures this dig."

"*Attendez. Attendez.* / One moment, please. You aren't employed at the dig?" Béchard scowled at his notes. "André Savard specifically said …"

I gave him what I hoped was my sweetest smile. "I'm spending my vacation volunteering at the dig. My real job is claims investigator for an international insurance company based in Boston." I crossed my fingers, hoping he'd be suitably impressed.

If he was, he didn't show it. "Unusual way to spend your vacation. But that's your business." He chewed his lower lip and studied me. "And this company for which you investigate…"

"New England Casualty and Indemnity." Oops! I had to stop interrupting the man if I wanted his cooperation.

"Quite a coincidence that they are insuring the dig where you volunteer, don't you agree?"

"Not at all. I learned about the dig at work. It sounded interesting. I had vacation time accumulated so I decided to volunteer. Now I need to get back to my day job."

Béchard gave me a quizzical look. "Your day job?"

"Investigating the claim."

"*Ah oui.*" He closed his eyes for a moment. "*Eh bien*, once you have provided me with your official papers—passport, visa and documentation that you have a right both to be at the dig and to conduct an investigation there—then you may do what you must. However, do nothing which interferes with, or in any way hinders, our official police investigation. Understood?"

I muttered, "Understood."

"Very well, then. What can you tell me about Michel Toussaint?"

"Not much, I'm sorry to say. This morning was to be my first day at work here."

"And when you reported today, the man was dead. So you had no chance to know him?"

"But I did meet him. Yesterday. I came by to see the dig. Toussaint was here. We spoke for a while."

Béchard's eyes widened. "Tell me more."

"I met him quite by chance." I gave the inspector the short version of my Sunday afternoon. "And then he was gone. Just like that." I snapped my fingers by way of demonstration.

"He had business elsewhere?"

"That's what he told me. He said he'd be gone until Wednesday. He also had an appointment yesterday. He left quickly, in a rush to get to it."

"He left here in a hurry, with no plans to be at the dig today. Yet here we find him. Dead. Where the man apparently did not intend to be." Béchard frowned yet again.

"That's right. And here I am at the scene of the accident. My company has a claim to process—perhaps more than one."

"*Comment*? / What? Has something else happened?"

"I overheard people talking this morning," I said, "about someone entering the dig's office during the night."

"Where is this office?"

"8 rue de Strasbourg."

He made an entry in his notebook. "So there was a break-in?"

"One of the archaeologists thought so. He was quite agitated." I thought for a moment. "But I didn't hear him say that anything had been taken or destroyed."

"His name?"

"I believe it is Claude."

"Can you describe him?"

I did my best with the physical description. "He was also distraught over the condition of the site where he had been working, the World War II area. He said the area had been vandalized. I don't know how anyone could be sure of that, given the condition of that area. Anyway, the man was visibly upset. I intend to seek him out later and see what I can learn."

"Isn't that my job?"

"It's mine as well, *Inspecteur*. My company will want a complete investigation before paying any claims."

"Which, as I have said, you may do once I have inspected your documents. Please come to the *Préfecture* in Paris tomorrow with your passport and visa. Then, investigate if you must. But again, I caution you: do nothing, say nothing, which might jeopardize the official investigation. Remain in contact with me. Keep me apprised of anything you learn."

I nodded and watched the stern look disappear from his face.

"As long your investigation does not interfere with police business, it would be my pleasure to assist you with your claim. I bid you good day." He handed me his business card, flashed an adorable smile and walked away.

I was right! Two gorgeous dimples. Not that it mattered. I was happily committed to Pete. Still, I couldn't help but notice.

There was little I could do here at the moment. I needed to call my office and alert them to the potential claims. I sought out André Savard to see what I should do about the next day. I'd decide later how to deal with my dual roles. The ideal would be to work on the dig while conducting my inquiries. No need to waste my vacation completely.

"Report to the office at 9:00," André told me. "By then we will have a better idea as to what to expect. If the police are finished at the site, we may possibly resume work as usual."

There may be work tomorrow, but it sure wouldn't be as usual. I shook my head and started toward the Métro station.

# Chapter 5

The train was nearly empty—too late for the morning rush, too early for the noontime crowds. It was my fourth ride on the Paris subway system, and the first time I actually had a seat. I closed my eyes and took a few deep breaths; time to relax and get my mind in gear.

The morning's events had been awful. My next move, calling into the office, could be equally unpleasant. My name was mud these days at NEC&I. My boss wasn't speaking to me. Nor were several co-workers who were covering for me for an entire month. My fault, of course. I never should have taken four weeks off in August. Never mind that I had earned every day of it. Or that, as the senior investigator, I got first dibs on time off.

Even old man Fisher, the president and CEO, had joined the fray, saying I had a lot of nerve taking an extended vacation and it set a bad example for the people who reported to me. I reminded him of the hours of unpaid overtime I had put in to keep up with the work the people who reported to me either bungled or didn't finish. He wasn't impressed.

And I was almost afraid to speak with Nancy.

She and I had been close friends since college. She helped me get my job in the claims department at NEC&I. She saw me through the terrible times after my fiancé Danny's death, stayed with me during the weeks after the funeral, helping me pull myself and my life back together. I helped her through the beginnings of her courtship with Mark Fisher, the son of the company's president.

Those days were long ago. Danny was gone three years now. Nancy was Mrs. Mark Fisher, an old married lady, working in Human Resources while trying to get pregnant. We hadn't spoken since that awful conversation in my office just before I left for Paris, when she tried to talk me out of going. Her voice was still booming in my ears ….

"I can't believe you're really doing this, Amy. Taking off for an entire month on some damn fool adventure. It's so unlike you. Leaving on barely a week's notice to get involved in God knows what."

"You know I've always wanted to work on a dig. The opportunity is finally here. And now. I can't pass it up."

"Taking so much time off is a deadly career move. Your boss looks like he can't handle something as simple as scheduling his staff's vacation time. You'll be lucky to have a job to come back to. Your co-workers will end up resenting you for being inconsiderate of their rights to time off. Honestly, Amy, this is a bad idea."

I couldn't argue with any of that, but for some reason it didn't matter. I let Nancy continue her tirade.

"And what do you really know about working on an archaeological dig?"

"Don't forget that I minored in archaeology in college."

"That was a while ago. And you've never actually worked on a dig before. God knows what you'll find there. It'll probably be awful."

She was right about that as well. I had no rebuttal. "I know what I read in the underwriting file. And it was a fluke that I ever saw it. Had to be karma. There it was one day. An underwriting file, sitting on my desk, with no explanation as to how it made its way to the Claims Department. As if the Universe knew I'd find it compelling. Everything happens for a reason. I was meant to see that file. Definitely karma."

"You're risking your career for a fluke?" Nancy was relentless. "It wasn't karma; it was just another mailroom screw-up. Come on, Amy, it's not too late to change your mind."

I knew I was beaten—and in the wrong. I took the time off anyway. I couldn't explain why, not even to myself. Nancy was right; this was not at all like me….

I'd call my administrative assistant Peggy instead.

I exited the Métro and headed to the rue du Four and the *pension* where I was living. A boarding house. Cheaper than a hotel. Breakfast and dinner included. And in the heart of Paris. Such a deal. I also thought I'd feel more secure there than in a hotel. Should anything untoward happen to me, at least someone would notice my absence.

Mme. Hulot, my landlady, was polishing the brass knocker on the carved wooden door. She was difficult not to notice—short and round, with hair dyed an amazing shade of red, dressed in a lavender flowered skirt and billowy pink blouse. She halted her work long enough to greet me, then resumed polishing with vigor.

The *pension* was quiet inside, the other boarders nowhere to be seen. That was fine. They weren't all that friendly. I hurried upstairs to the corner room which was my home for the next month. The room was compact—one bed, slightly smaller than the average American twin, cheap flowered cotton spread, a small wooden table with one chair, a larger chair made of stained artificial leather and an armoire. No bureau, no closet, just an armoire. A small alcove off to one side contained a sink and a bidet. A communal toilet and shower were down the hall. Not luxurious, but good enough.

I checked my watch. With the time difference, the office wouldn't open for nearly three hours. What to do with the time? No question, no contest, no debate. Jet lag made the decision for me. I set the alarm and closed my eyes for a nap.

A few hours later, a knock on the door awakened me. "Who is it?"

"*C'est moi* / It is I, Madame Hulot. A surprise has arrived for you."

I opened the door to see her holding a vase of long-stemmed red roses. Obviously from Pete. He loved to give me roses. The card said, "Hope you're having a wonderful time. Wish I was there." Sweet.

I fished my cell phone out of my shoulder bag to call and thank him, only to discover the phone was dead. I'd forgotten to charge the damn thing. And I couldn't find the charger cord or the electrical adapter. No time to look now. They'd turn up later.

In need of a Plan B, I sought out Henrique, the male half of the Portuguese couple who worked at the *pension*. "Please. I would like to use the telephone. Is that all right?"

"*Certainement, Mademoiselle*." His French came with a thick Portuguese accent. He was short and squat, with thick, dark, curly hair. "Any charges you incur will be billed to you at the end of the week. Wait in the dining room, *s'il vous plaît*. I will fetch the key." And off he went.

The key? What was that all about? I found the answer soon enough when I entered the dining room. An old-fashioned black telephone with a rotary dial, like the one my grandmother used to have, sat on a table in a corner. I hadn't noticed it before. The phone had to be at least fifty years old. A small padlock was fastened to the rotary dial, preventing any unauthorized use.

Henrique returned with a small key and unlocked the dial.

I consulted my guidebook on the intricacies of international calls, then dialed Pete. The call went directly to voice mail. Bummer. I left a quick voicemail and planned to try again later.

In the meantime, I needed to speak with my office. One ring, two rings, three rings. Why didn't Peggy answer?

"Hello. This is Nancy Fisher. May I help you?"

"Nancy?" *Damn!*

"Amy?"

"It's me. What's going on? Where's Peggy?"

"At the dentist. Shall I have her call you?"

"Never mind that. Why are you answering her phone?"

Nancy let out a long, noisy sigh. "I'm filling in, helping out in Claims for a while. You know how it gets in the summer. Everybody taking vacations, always being short-handed."

Ouch! "That sounds like a dig—one aimed directly at me." And I deserved it.

"Sorry. I'm a bit stressed. It's a circus here. Why are you calling? Are you about to tell me you've had enough of digging up the past and will be on the next plane home?"

I pretended not to hear the snarl in her voice. "No, but you and I need to talk. You're my best friend. I hate having you upset with me."

"Listen, Amy, I'm sorry for the way I over-reacted to your vacation plans. I had other things on my mind. You threw a major monkey wrench at me."

"Can we please be friends again?"

"Of course we can."

That was a relief. "You had a right to say what you did, Nance. It's all true. I have no defense, except perhaps for temporary insanity."

"So you're not coming home?"

"Sorry, not yet."

"In that case, how is Paris?"

"What I've seen of it so far is either elegant and beautiful or charming and quaint. The city is amazingly clean, the gardens are delightful. Cafés and boutiques are everywhere. The air smells like freshly baked bread." I didn't mention the negative things, like the never-ending noise of the traffic or the ubiquitous odor of diesel fuel. That could wait for another time. "But more about that later. Believe it or not, this is a business call."

"I don't follow you."

"I'm giving you a heads-up on a claim." A sigh escaped me.

"Come again?"

I filled her in on recent events at the dig, and the few facts I knew so far. It didn't take long. "If I do a bang-up job investigating this, maybe I can redeem myself at the office. What do you think?"

"It's worth a shot. Lord knows you're not too popular around here at the moment. Mitch is still fuming at you for taking off on short notice and making him look like the idiot that he is. Even my father-in-law is still sputtering about your absence, asking if I've heard from you. A few weeks ago he didn't even know your name. And now you're at the top of his shit list."

"I get it, Nance. I messed up. People are angry. But I can make up for all that by investigating this claim."

"Exactly how are you going to manage that? You don't know the ropes in France. You have no connections. What about cooperation from the local authorities? You're going to need that big time."

I let out a slight giggle. "Piece of cake."

"Because …?"

"I met the detective assigned to investigate Toussaint's death. I just came from discussing the case with him." No point in mentioning how attractive the man was. Nancy didn't need to know that.

"Way to go, Amy. You may be able to pull this off after all. Maybe you were meant to be there, meant to meet that detective. Like you said. Karma and all that. So, let's get down to business. Tell me about the fellow who died. What's his name again?"

"Toussaint. Michel Toussaint." I spelled it. "He is—or was—the head archaeologist."

"Was he in charge? Or working for someone else?"

"I'm not sure. Shouldn't that information be in the file?"

"It should. But it could be a few days before I can lay my hands on the paper file. The file clerk's on vacation. The girl who's filling in is a waste of skin. She'd fit right in working in the mail room, if you know what I mean."

I knew only too well. "What about the computer records?"

"I'm looking now. The trouble is the data entry department is months behind schedule with the new database. Apparently their people have been on vacation lately too. Damn this new software anyway. I'm getting only bare bones information here."

"I'll see what I can learn on this end." And I'd begin with Marie Duprès.

"Sounds good. Keep me posted on everything you learn. I'll put in a good word for you with Mitch. For dedication above and beyond the call of duty, working during your vacation. How's that?"

"Works for me. For now, I'll go back to the worksite and see what I can dig up."

Nancy groaned. She hated my bad puns.

"I'll get you copies of the police and coroner's reports as soon as they're available. Can you tell me if we're writing full coverage on the dig? We may not even be covering the vandalism loss."

There was a moment of international silence.

"Here we go," Nancy spoke up. "St. Denis Archaeological Dig. Workers' Comp, of course, and on-site liability coverage. Some property coverage, but it's very limited."

"How so?"

"We're only covering artifacts once they've been removed and studied and had a value placed on them. No property coverage for work in progress at the site. No surprise there. Also no coverage for the dig sites themselves. Property coverage at the office includes the building and its contents, for the usual array of perils. Deductible is $5,000 or 5,000 euros, whichever is more at the moment."

I made notes as she spoke. "Dynamite. That'll help a lot. I'll call again soon with any new information I have. I'll fax the reports when I get them."

"Great." Nancy paused. "I'm sorry about your vacation."

"I'll deal with it. Should I be sorry for your temporary demotion back to Claims?"

She laughed. "No way. It's actually a nice respite. I'm loving being away from that old coot upstairs for a while. He gives me the creeps."

"You mean your father-in-law?"

"I sure do. Can't explain why, but I don't like the man. He makes me uncomfortable. Always has."

"Yet you married Mark anyway."

"What can I say? I didn't expect to be working in such close proximity to the old man. Figured he'd retire, Mark would become president and CEO and we'd live happily ever after."

"How old is Fisher anyway?"

"Got to be around eighty. Maybe older. And in good health. Creepy, but healthy."

"He's old enough to be Mark's grandfather."

"That's for sure."

"What does Mark say about him?"

"I can't discuss my feelings about him with Mark. The man's his dad." Nancy paused.

I heard somebody speaking in the background.

"Listen, Amy, I've got to go. Things are getting wild around here. Call me tomorrow."

After she'd hung up I realized I hadn't asked her what had been so heavy on her mind the day of our argument.

# Chapter 6

I awoke early the next morning to a battle brewing in my head: report to the dig as an eager volunteer or confess my true identity and mission? Pondering my conundrum, I breakfasted on coffee, hot and strong, and half a loaf of fresh, crusty bread, split and buttered—what Danny used to call a *tartine*. The bread was the stuff of which dreams are made, still warm from the baker's oven. Standard morning fare at the *pension*. Not even my present dilemma could keep me from savoring my morning meal.

In the end, I reached a decision of sorts, where neither side won—or lost. I could fulfill both roles at once; working at the dig could only help me sort out the claim. I would be up-front about my day job. As much as I wanted to lose myself in my archaeological vacation, this was the right thing to do. Marie Duprès could decide what to tell the others. I knew this was passing the buck, but it felt right.

Confident I could make this arrangement work, I decided to be prepared. André Savard had said work might resume at the dig site. I dressed in my digger's clothes: cut-off jeans and my favorite T-shirt. It said, "Star Fleet Academy" and was beginning to look seedy. Brand new sneakers completed the ensemble. I stowed my passport, visa and NEC&I ID card in my shoulder bag, planning to stop by the police station in the afternoon. And today I didn't forget my camera.

With my cell phone now charged, I dialed my boyfriend Pete. When I'd called the other day to let him know I'd arrived safely and to thank him for the roses, I had to settle for voice mail. Today I wanted to hear *his* voice. It had a magical quality which could always cheer me up—or calm me down. No luck today. Voice mail again. Maybe he was sleeping.

Leaving another message, I started off to the dig's office on the rue de Strasbourg, eager to meet Marie Duprès.

I frowned when I arrived at the building which housed the office. On a street lined with century-old tumble-down wood frame buildings, this was by far the worst, a sad and tired sight. The paint was faded and peeling. Had it once been blue? The windows were in need of a good washing. One was cracked in two places, another was boarded up. This was the main office for a government-sponsored archaeological dig? Had the Underwriting Department seen a photo of this place before writing the coverage? I shook my head and rang the doorbell. It didn't work. The door was ajar. I walked in to search for Marie Duprès.

Nobody was in any of the four small rooms on the ground floor. Nothing there but clutter and the smell of mold. Wheelbarrows, crates and buckets filled with shovels and assorted tools were everywhere. A large supply of well-used toothbrushes sat on a beat-up old table.

The sound of footsteps echoed from the floor above. I called "*Bonjour*" and started up the stairs. The steps creaked beneath even my insubstantial weight.

"*Qui est-ce*?" a female voice responded. "Who is it?"

"Amy Lynch. I'm looking for Marie Duprès."

"And here you find her."

A small frail-looking woman of at least 80 appeared at the top of the stairs. She had short, straight gray hair and leathery skin. And incredible eyes! A beautiful soft blue, very round, full of life, and absolutely sparkling despite signs of recent tears.

Marie held out her hand. “It is a pleasure to make your acquaintance. I only regret that we meet under such sad circumstances.” She choked back a sob. A single tear made its way down her cheek. She made no attempt to wipe it away.

“It’s good to meet you, Marie.” I joined her at the top of the stairs and shook her outstretched hand. Her fingers were gnarled and twisted. A painful sight. I smiled and focused on her wonderful dancing eyes. “I’m so very sorry about M. Toussaint.”

“*Ah, oui*. We all are. Such a tragedy.”

“Will there be work on the site today? Have the police completed their investigation?”

Marie smiled. “I have just finished speaking with them. They informed me that they will continue their investigation of the pit where Michel was found. We may resume our work on both the habitation and the gravesite as long as we avoid the pit and do not interfere with their work.”

This should have been the moment to discuss my true role with Marie. I opened my mouth to do so when the front door banged and the sounds of footsteps and muted conversation interrupted my effort.

“The others are arriving,” Marie said. “Come. I will introduce you.”

We headed down the stairs.

Three men and one woman stood in the entryway—the oldest probably not yet twenty-five. André was among them. I recognized the woman from the mob scene the day before. Her eyes were puffy, and more than a little blood-shot. The men were dressed in blue overalls with no shirts beneath, the woman in cut-off jeans and a “Sorbonne” T-shirt.

Marie greeted them. “*Mes amis*, this is a sad day. The death of Michel Toussaint is a terrible blow to us all.”

The woman sobbed softly. The others nodded.

"We are all devastated," Marie continued. "But we must not dwell on our sadness. We must now honor Michel's memory by continuing his work. He would want it so. Being busy will help ease our grief. Work is a medicine necessary to us all." She looked in my direction. "I am pleased to introduce to you *Mademoiselle* Amy Lynch from America. She has been kind enough to volunteer her services to us for the month of August. Amy, this is Pierre, Solange, Georges and André."

I catalogued them in my mind as potential witnesses—or possible suspects. Each of them shook my hand and mumbled words of welcome. The woman, Solange, scowled ever-so-slightly. André winked and said, "A pleasure to see you again." Then all eight eyes turned to Marie.

"The police have completed their examination of the worksite," Marie announced. "We are now free to resume our work, except for the deepest pit, the one where … where …." She took a deep breath, her fingers trembling. "We have very little staff today, so we will concentrate our efforts on two small areas. Pierre, Solange and Georges, you will work on the gravesite. You know what must be done. André, you and Amy will address the 12th century habitation area. I trust you can direct and assist her as needed. *Bon courage, mes amis*. The work will be a tonic for us all." She turned and mounted the stairs.

My co-diggers erupted into a flurry of movement, grabbing buckets from a pile on the floor and filling them with a variety of brushes, dustpans, tiny trowels—all the tools of the trade.

André filled a second bucket and offered it to me. "*Eh bien, mes amis*, let us follow Marie's brave example. Shall we be off?"

# Chapter 7

So there we were, pushing wheelbarrows and carrying buckets up the streets of St. Denis. André took up the rear with me. "Your French is quite good."

"I used to live in Québec. Taught school there for a few years."

"That explains your charming accent. What did you teach?"

"English."

André fished out his keys as we neared the gate to the site. "You have studied archaeology?"

"Yes, but this is my first dig. I hope you don't mind."

"Not a problem," he grinned. "My job is to teach you."

"Who taught you?" I asked. "Michel Toussaint?"

"*Ah, non*. The work at St. Denis is my first dig with Michel. *Évidemment* I have learned much from the man, but my prior experience was in the Midi, the South of France."

"Were you and Michel friends?"

"More like colleagues. He was a single-minded individual. Our conversations dealt primarily with our work."

So much for gaining insight from André. Perhaps I'd learn more from the others.

As we entered the work site, Pierre, Georges and Solange walked over to the grave area as if in a trance. I watched them avert their eyes from the large pit, now empty of Toussaint's body. The area was cordoned off with police tape. The police investigators working there didn't acknowledge our arrival.

André led me to the twelfth century habitation area and handed me a bucket. "These are your tools for the day. Here you have brushes of various sizes and intensities. They are for cleaning the foundation. All remaining debris must be removed from the area. Bear in mind that debris consists of anything and everything you find, including dirt, if it is found on the stone foundation. Collect the debris with the dustpan and brush and place it in this container." He held up a red tin box.

I accepted the box and awaited further instructions.

"This box will be marked with the location where the material was found, as well as the date and your name, then returned for study. This is the manner in which you will spend your day. Shall we begin?"

The area didn't look anything like a house—or a habitation. More like a concrete-lined hole in the ground surrounded by walls. A wooden ladder stood waiting for us to descend to the bottom, around seven or eight feet down. I climbed down first. André passed tools down to me, one by one. I was pleased he left the wheelbarrow on the upper surface.

André came down the ladder, led me to one corner and showed me how to begin. He then retreated to the opposite corner and began making diagrams of the area.

So, I was going to spend the day alone, on my knees, cleaning dirt, pretending I hadn't seen a dead man in the pit less than 15 feet away. And having minimal contact or conversation with the others. Not what I had envisioned. Nothing at all like the adventures of Indiana Jones. And not particularly conducive to learning much about Michel Toussaint. Part of me rejoiced at the prospect of spending a beautiful summer day performing a mindless task. Part of me worked at conjuring up excuses to speak with the others, with little success. Within no time, I relaxed and let my mind wander.

For better or worse, my first thought was of Pete—and of the fact that I didn't deserve him. He'd been so supportive of my hasty decision to leave him for a month abroad when he had to bow out at the last minute. A lesser man would have asked me to wait until he could accompany me. "It sounds wonderful," he told me. "Go. Enjoy yourself. Just call me regularly to let me know how it's going. I'll miss you, but I'll be fine knowing you're doing something that makes you happy."

And here I was, taking full advantage of his good nature and expecting him to welcome me with open arms when I returned. But what if he didn't? He'd been a bit off lately, sort of distant and cool. I had assumed he was just tired, but what if I was wrong? Maybe he'd decided I wasn't the love of his life after all? Maybe a short break would help us figure out our relationship, where it was going, where we wanted it to go.

André stopped by regularly to check my progress. He was helpful and encouraging, as if the job I was doing actually mattered. Late in the morning, he had me stop work while he photographed the area. "Documentation is made at each stage of excavation. Detailed notes are crucial because, in order to do a thorough study of a site, one must dismantle that site in the process. Photos are taken from all conceivable angles. Maps and charts and diagrams are drawn." He moved about the area as he spoke, snapping photos from a variety of angles.

"Why the drawings and diagrams?" I asked. "Wouldn't photos be sufficient?"

"*Ah, non.* One must account for the sun."

"The sun?"

"*Oui*, and the shadows. In a photo, it can be difficult to differentiate between shadows and areas which are, in fact, darker than others. The darker shades often denote the beginning of a new layer, a different material, a separate period in time."

"Interesting. Thanks for the lesson."

"*De rien.* / You're welcome. Come. Let us see how the others are progressing. It is nearly time for lunch."

I followed him up the ladder and toward the gravesite.

Pierre was busy brushing soil from a skeleton. Each move seemed calculated to remove as little as possible. Solange sat quietly sketching another of the bodies. She used gridded graph paper, stopping frequently to measure the bones, then the grids, then to do some math. Georges stood apart from the others, taking photos of the area. I watched for a bit, then addressed Pierre. "What will you do with these remains once they've been uncovered, drawn and photographed?"

"They will be removed with great care and dignity, studied at the rue de Strasbourg, then re-buried locally—with reverence."

His haughty tone suggested I should have known this already. Nobody else volunteered any information. Professional snobbery at its best.

We broke for lunch at noon, as announced by the bells of the Basilica of St. Denis. Solange and Georges gathered their tools and prepared to leave. Not the friendliest of co-workers. Perhaps they were nice people who were simply in shock.

André locked the dig site and headed out. I followed him through alleyways devoid of sun and side streets lined with ramshackle houses. We ended up at a small school building. Entering the cafeteria, I saw five people already there, seated at a table.

"These are others from the dig," André told me. "They have been working at the office with Marie this morning. We lunch together here. As the government is responsible for the dig, they provide meals for the diggers." He led me to a table.

Lunch was a morbid affair. Sad faces all around. The occasional tear. Nobody spoke above a whisper, and then only when necessary. I was a lost soul. André was seated far enough from me to make conversation impossible. Nobody else acknowledged my existence. I attributed that to their grief rather than to something I might have said or done.

I tried to strike up a conversation with the woman next to me. Hope springs eternal. "This meat is excellent. What is it?"

"It is tongue. *Délicieux, n'est-ce pas*? And the sauce has a very good taste." She took another bite.

I stared at my plate in horror—though I had to admit that the sauce did indeed have a very good taste.

Nobody lingered once the meal was finished. They rose to leave. I followed half a beat behind the others. They walked right past the locked gate of the dig site.

"Aren't we going back to work?" I asked André, who had moved beside me.

"Eventually. But first we return to the office where we take our midday coffee."

Entering the building on the rue de Strasbourg, we went through to a small open courtyard in the center. Marie had coffee waiting for us, which, oddly enough, we drank from small glasses while seated on wooden benches. Marie was everywhere at once, speaking with everyone, checking on their progress, catching up on the day's activities, apparently working hard at a semblance of normalcy. Her efforts to cheer the others worked, at least a little.

Glasses empty, the crew rose and proceeded to a large table in the rear of the courtyard. Standing around the table, each person picked up a toothbrush. I held back, unsure what to expect.

André and Marie appeared with a large bucket filled with many strange items, most of them small, all of them covered with a thin layer of dirt. Marie placed this in the center of the table between two large bowls of water. Each person pulled something from the bucket and began to clean it with a toothbrush. I followed suit.

We stood at the table cleaning the tiny artifacts. There was little conversation at first. Marie returned to her office after a few minutes. Then the speculations began.

A short young man with a Slavic look spoke first. "It is no wonder Michel fell to his death, *vous savez*. He had worked himself into a state of exhaustion these past few weeks. This is what causes accidents like this. Trying to do everything too well and too fast. All to satisfy the whims of bureaucrats who give us too little time to do too much."

Feigning interest in the artifact I was cleaning, I took in every word.

A girl to my left shook her head. "*Mais non.* It wasn't exhaustion. It was Michel's excitement over that strange old note Claude unearthed last week."

My ears perked up. "What kind of note? Was it buried at the dig site?" I asked of nobody in particular. And why was Michel Toussaint excited about it? This could be a good starting point in my investigation.

"Nobody knows," André told me. "Claude showed it to Marie and Michel. They spirited it away. Said they were going to investigate further before saying anything, or showing anybody. It was so unlike them to keep secrets like that. But Michel couldn't hide his excitement. I'm certain he returned to the site, alone, to investigate further. It was dark. And *voilà*, he fell to his death."

Solange slammed a toothbrush onto the table and glared at André. "Fell! How can you even think such a thing? Does anybody believe that Michel would be so careless? His fall was obviously deliberate." She folded her arms across her chest and glared at everybody.

Pierre's eyes widened. "*Mon Dieu.* Are you suggesting that he jumped?"

"That shouldn't surprise you," Solange responded. "He had been terribly depressed lately. Over problems with his grant. And with … other things as well."

"What was the problem with the grant?" George asked.

"People at the Ministry have been making things difficult for Michel. Threatening to cut off his funding. Damn the government." She sniffled.

"What are you saying, Solange? Why on earth would they do that? The work has been progressing nicely. We have uncovered so much of interest."

"It was something political. It had to be. They were giving him a very hard time. He was depressed." She collapsed into tears.

Nobody jumped to comfort Solange, or to rally to her cause.

"Maybe he surprised drug dealers and they pushed him. There has been talk of drug activity in the neighborhood," someone suggested.

And on it went.

Around mid-afternoon, the sky darkened and the rain began with a vengeance. Marie emerged from her office and announced that the outside work had ended for the day. No point trying to continue in this weather. She approached me on my way out of the courtyard. "Tomorrow morning, André must complete photographing the habitation area where you worked this morning. While he does this, you and I will make a small excursion, to the *Musée Municipale d'Art et d'Histoire,* where we display our artifacts and explain the history and significance of the site. I will show you the results of our work at St. Denis over the past several years. This knowledge will give you more perspective on the work you are doing."

"That sounds wonderful. But wouldn't you rather leave it for later? This is such a difficult time for you."

Marie shook her head. "The only way to cope with grief is to work through it. Showing you the museum will be of help to me. And you will benefit from seeing the historical context of the artifacts we have catalogued so that when you find something at the work site, you will know what is of importance and requires extra care. Also, I will appreciate the opportunity to know you better. We can have a nice long chat."

And I would have the opportunity to come clean with Marie and discuss the claim. "All right, then."

"*Bon*. Shall we meet at 9:30? The museum is not far from here, on the rue Gabriel Péri."

"That would be wonderful."

I headed for the Métro station a bit worse for the wear—dirty, sweaty and more than a little tired. Trudging down the street in the rain, I was eager to record and ponder everything I'd just heard. Not to mention the opportunity for some alone time with Marie tomorrow. The woman had an aura of mystery about her, as if she was protecting a secret.

# Chapter 8

# Judas - Far from France 2003

Judas's hands shook as he reached for the phone to call his son in France. He cursed the fate that had brought him to this point. That damn note, found after all these years. The bombs hadn't destroyed his dead drop after all.

"Allô, Philippe. Did you succeed?"

"Of course I did, Papa. Just as you instructed. Moreau is dead. He can no longer threaten you. You are safe from him, and no one will ever question his death."

Moreau, the trusted friend, his only link to the past. Moreau—who had always believed Judas's lies, who helped him escape from France—had become his mortal enemy. How could a piece of paper change somebody so?

"Did you retrieve the note from him before he died?"

"Mais oui, Papa, just as you asked. Moreau gave me his copy of the note."

"His copy!"Judas bellowed. "What do you mean his copy?"

"It was all the man had. The archaeologist kept the original."

"And did you deal with the archaeologist as well?"

*"Bien sûr* / Of course. He is dead as well."

"Did you obtain the note from him first?"

"Hélas, that I could not do. He refused to deal with me."

"And yet you killed him? Why, Philippe? Why?"

"It could not be helped, Papa. He refused to be reasonable."

"Did he tell you where the note is?"

"Sadly, no."

"So we are no better off than before." Judas growled.

"I did what I could, Papa. I did what I could."

Judas fumed and slammed down the phone. What kind of child had he sired? Philippe was nothing but an incompetent fool who acted out of impulse, who didn't think.

Moreau was no longer a threat, but Judas was still not safe. At least one copy of the note still existed—maybe more. He couldn't rest until they were all destroyed.

Judas cursed the fates again and struggled to figure out how to get his hands on the note. Only then could he rest.

# Chapter 9

The route to the Métro station led past the two dig sites on the rue Jean Jaurès. As I passed, I replayed the scene from the day before, with the lifeless body at the bottom of the pit.

Barely twenty-four hours later, work, albeit limited, had resumed. The atmosphere was subdued, true, and the area where the body was found was cordoned off, but still, how disrespectful it seemed. A man was dead. A cold shiver made its way slowly down my back; a tear ran down my cheek; the rain poured down on my head.

"Good afternoon, *Mademoiselle*. I am pleased to meet you again."

I spun around to see Béchard, the police detective who had interviewed me yesterday, the one with the wonderful dimples. He was wearing the same suit, and the same shirt. At least the tie was different, this one all greens and blues. He still had his man-purse.

"How nice to see you again, *Inspecteur*." And I wasn't just mouthing pleasantries.

"Has the rain ended your digging for the day?"

"Yes. I was actually on my way to the Paris police station, to provide you with my passport and other documents."

He pursed his lips. “It appears I may save you that trip. I am on my way to interview people at the dig office. The initial reports provided to me by the other policemen at the scene of Toussaint’s death are seriously inadequate. *Hélas*, if one wants a job done properly, it is necessary to do it one’s self.” He sighed.

“I know what you mean.”

“Perhaps I should begin with you, *Mademoiselle*. If you have some time at your disposal, would you be good enough to spend a bit of it with me to follow up on the information you provided yesterday? At the same time, I can verify your documents.”

“My pleasure, *Inspecteur*.” *Particularly if you’d smile again and show me those dimples.*

“*C’est bon* / Good. But let us not continue our discussion in this dismal place. May I offer you a coffee?” He gestured up the street toward the Métro. “I know a café in the Place Hugo. We would be more comfortable there. And drier.” His eyes strayed to my Star Fleet Academy T-shirt, now sopping wet and clingy.

I pretended not to notice. “Sounds like just what the doctor ordered.”

He knit his brow. “The doctor?”

“An American expression. It means I’d love some coffee.” I took a last look at the deserted site, then walked up the street with Béchard. I began a few steps behind him, just out of curiosity. I was right: nice buns.

We chose a small table by the window in the café, affording an excellent view of the Basilica of St. Denis, one of the more famous churches in the area. We ordered coffee.

I studied the basilica across the street, named for St. Denis, a French martyr. The kings of France came here to be married. Odd—it had only one tower. Was the other destroyed in the war?

Béchard interrupted my thoughts. "I regret you will see no weddings here today. While many couples wish to be married in the same church as the kings of France, they may do so only on weekends."

So much for gawking. Time for business.

I showed him my papers, which he studied intently, and with a furrowed brow. He made notes. I held my breath throughout this process. He had to accept them as genuine and allow me to investigate. My job might depend on it.

After an eternity, he looked up and smiled. "Your documents appear to be in order."

*Whew!*

He looked at my passport again. "So, you are from Massachusetts?"

"That's right. I live in Cambridge, just outside of Boston."

"Is that anywhere near Woods Hole?"

Interesting question. "Not far. Actually, Woods Hole is part of Falmouth, where I grew up. Why do you ask?"

"I have a friend who works in Woods Hole. He is an oceanographer."

"You're kidding me."

"Why would I wish to do that?"

"It's such a coincidence. I used to work in Woods Hole summers when I was in college. What's your friend's name? Maybe I know him."

"Étienne Dumont."

I shook my head. "The name doesn't ring a bell."

He gave me a quizzical look. "Ring a bell?"

"An American expression. It means the name doesn't sound familiar. If you give me his information, I can look him up when I get home."

He tore a page from his notebook, wrote his friend's name and handed it to me along with my papers.

I assumed that meant I could work with him. "How is your investigation progressing?"

"As you say, it is my investigation. It is I who will be asking the questions."

Apparently I was mistaken. Properly chastised, I remained silent while he consulted his notes.

"What was the purpose of the beam we found at the bottom of the pit?" he asked.

"To cross the pit. The ladder to descend into the work area was kept on the other side."

"Isn't that location somewhat inconvenient?"

"Deliberately so. The archaeologists reduce traffic over the work in progress by discouraging people from entering the pit unless truly necessary."

"Interesting idea." He scanned his notes, then spoke more to himself than to me. "This beam was approximately six meters long, thirty centimeters wide and fifteen centimeters thick. Indications are that the side supports, composed of gravel and stone, had eroded sufficiently so as to cause the beam to give way as Toussaint crossed."

I shook my head. "That scenario doesn't make sense."

He raised his brows. "What does not make sense?"

"The idea that the beam gave way. The dig officials would, or should, have had adequate safety measures in place."

"*Ah, oui*. I see what you mean."

Our coffees arrived. We fell silent as we sipped.

Béchard put down his cup and said, "Do you recall the condition of this beam when you visited the site with Toussaint on Sunday?"

"I didn't get all that close to the pit. Sorry."

"Was there any discussion at the dig today that may shed some light on what happened?"

His question provided me with my big chance. I leaned toward him. "I'll make a deal with you. If I tell you everything I heard from the other diggers, will you make it easier for me to get the information I need for my claim?"

He mulled this over. "*Eh bien, oui.* That would be an equitable exchange. Let us begin by exchanging telephone numbers."

We accomplished this quickly, then I filled him in on the conversations in the courtyard and the various theories put forth—accident, suicide, murder.

He made copious notes. "Do you believe Toussaint's death was an accident?"

"It's possible, but I don't think so. As I told you, the beam should have been better secured. And would a man really die from a fall of twenty feet, especially if he landed on a pile of soil?

"Feet I do not understand. But I see what you mean. Do you believe Toussaint killed himself?"

"It would be a strange way to commit suicide. Why loosen the beam first? Why not simply jump? And again, would he die from such a short fall? One would think he would choose a method more likely to produce the desired result."

"You may be right. But what alternatives remain? Do you believe he was pushed?"

I shuddered. "Such a terrible thought. I don't know." I took a large gulp of my coffee.

He scribbled more notes. After a few moments, he put the notebook down and smiled at me. "I shall check with the local police about possible criminal activity in the area. In the meantime, *s'il vous plaît*, tell me what makes an insurance investigator from America decide to volunteer on an archaeological dig in St. Denis."

The man was a master of mixed signals. I didn't mind. "I studied archaeology in college and had always wanted to work at a dig. Last month, the opportunity fell into my lap."

"Fell into your lap?" A puzzled look crossed his face.

"Presented itself unexpectedly. As I told you yesterday, I learned of the dig at work. The information in the file piqued my interest. I had vacation time coming. I volunteered. Slave labor in exchange for practical experience and training. And here I am." After the uproar my departure had caused, I only wished coming here had actually been that simple.

"Does the dig provide you with lodging as well? And meals?"

"It does. But I chose to stay at a *pension* in the city instead. To be in the heart of Paris." I gave him the name and address of my home away from home.

"I am familiar with this neighborhood. Are you pleased with your choice?"

"So far, yes."

"And—you are not feeling homesick I hope?"

Our conversation was beginning to get personal. I answered him anyway, to keep on his good side. "I haven't had much time to think about home. So much is happening here. I do miss Sam, though."

"Sam is your husband?"

I laughed. "I'm not married. Sam is my dog. Also my best friend. I miss him very much. We have wonderful, long conversations. He's an excellent listener."

Béchard shrugged his shoulders. "Who is caring for Sam in your absence?"

"A friend of mine who has a nice yard." As I finished my now-tepid coffee, something occurred to me. "Was a flashlight found in or near the pit?"

Béchard grinned. "*Ah, non*, no flashlight. And so, *mon amie* Amy, the plot becomes more thick. We now have a case which presents some interest. Do you not agree?"

"If you mean, what was Toussaint doing there in the middle of the night without a flashlight, I most certainly do agree."

He checked his watch. "I must now interview the other workers from the dig before returning to the station in Paris to work on my report." He hesitated, then added, "What will you do for the rest of the day?"

"Return to the *pension* to change my clothes. I shouldn't be parading around Paris in this outfit." I frowned down at my cut-offs and Star Trek T-shirt.

"Do not be so sure." He smiled. "May I escort you to the Métro?"

As we headed up the street, Béchard said, "My office is but a short distance from your *pension*, at the *Préfecture de Police* on the *Île de la Cité*. Perhaps you would consent to dine with me some evening?"

I hesitated, then said "That would be very nice." Pete and I weren't married. We weren't engaged. And *Inspecteur Béchard* was both charming and adorable. So why was I feeling so guilty?

# Chapter 10

I said very little during dinner that evening. I couldn't shut my mind off long enough to be sociable. Not that it mattered. My fellow boarders scarcely noticed me. The three Japanese girls chatted amongst themselves. The two Germans were absent. The Frenchman just sat and stared at his bottle of wine. Was he afraid somebody might ask him to share it? Nevertheless, it was better than eating alone in a restaurant.

I ate quickly and prepared to go out. It was a lovely, mild evening. A walk and a nice glass of wine would do me good. Strolling up the Boulevard Saint Germain, I found a café that was inviting and not crowded. Gypsies in colorful garb were dancing on the sidewalk nearby. The perfect place to relax and soak up the atmosphere. Sitting at an outdoor table, I ordered a glass of wine and began to relax and enjoy the entertainment.

My phone rang as my wine arrived. Caller ID said it was Peggy, my administrative assistant, good friend and dog sitter. "Hello to you," I said.

"If my calculations are correct, it's 9:00 PM in Paris. Please tell me you're out and about and enjoying yourself."

"You can count on it. What's up?"

"Just checking in. How's Paris?"

"It's a wonderful city." I ran through all the lovely things I'd mentioned to Nancy, then added, "The traffic is beyond noisy and the streets stink of diesel fuel. But I can live with that."

"And how's that place where you're living? What did you call it – a *pension*?"

"It's fine."

"Do you like the people there?"

I sighed. "They're not very sociable, but that's all right. I'm comfortable with my own company." I didn't mention that of Béchard.

I waited to hear the real reason for her call. Peggy was never one for idle chit-chat.

"Sorry I missed your call yesterday. Nancy was just here and filled me in on what happened at the dig. How awful," Peggy said.

"And then some.  How's Sam?" My scruffy mutt and best friend was spending the month with Peggy. Maybe he was the reason for her call.

"Great. He's such a good boy. And you're right, he is a wonderful listener."

"Does he miss me?"

"Of course. But he was happy when Pete stopped by the other day. The two of them had a nice long walk."

"Pete stopped by? How was he?"

"Fine."

"What did he want?"

"Nothing really. I think being with Sam made him less lonesome for you. You really hit the jackpot with him, Amy. Guys like that are hard to find."

I hoped she was right. I didn't tell her about his recent behavior or my potential date with Béchard.  So Sam wasn't the reason for her call, nor was Pete. "What's been happening at the office?"

"Not much, except for old man Fisher throwing a major nutty this morning—in your direction."

"What? Why? Has he joined the 'I hate Amy Lynch because she took a month-long vacation' club?"

"I think so. And the fact that you're working at an archaeological dig sent him right over the edge."

"What does he care what I do with my time off?"

"He says it's wrong to dig up the past. What's done is done and should remain buried, whatever the heck that means."

"Did you defend me?"

"I tried. Don't think it did much good. Sorry."

We had an awkward silence. Whatever else Peggy had to tell me, it couldn't be good.

"Let's get back to Nancy," I prompted. "She waited a whole day to tell you what happened here. That's not like her."

"I know. That's actually why I called. Nancy has been a bit pre-occupied lately, not quite herself."

"Please don't tell me it's because of that dreadful argument she and I had."

"Not exactly. But there is something you need to know."

The tone of Peggy's voice told me this 'something' wasn't good. "What do you mean?"

"The day you announced your vacation plans, Nancy was about to tell you she was pregnant. Then she got so upset with you, she decided not to."

"Pregnant! That's wonderful news. I'm so happy for her." And relieved the news wasn't bad. "Why didn't she tell me when we spoke yesterday? She must be so excited. I'd expect her to be telling everybody."

"She miscarried last week."

I nearly dropped my phone. "Oh, no. That's awful. I could die for her. She wants a baby so bad. Has for so long. Losing it must be dreadfully hard on her. How is she handling it? Why isn't she taking time off?" I stopped speaking long enough to give Peggy time to answer.

"Nancy's tougher than you think, Amy. She'll work through her pain. Just give her time."

"What she needs is love and a lot of TLC. Can you give her some in my absence? I'll call her this evening to see how she's doing." And to apologize for not being there when my best friend needed me.

I rang off from Peggy, hurried back to the *pension* and called Nancy.

We had a heartfelt chat and a good long cry together. She said she was sad, but coping, and always hopeful of becoming pregnant again soon. I was sad for my friend. I promised to keep in touch regularly, then slipped into a restless sleep. I was antsy about my meeting with Marie in the morning, and telling her the truth about me.

# Chapter 11

My stomach was doing flip-flops as I arrived at the *Musée Municipale d'Art et d'Histoire*. The time had come to reveal my true identity. I wasn't sure how Marie would react.

Marie was waiting on a bench outside the museum, an old two-story white stone structure. She jumped up to greet me. "*Bonjour, mon amie*. You are right on time."

"What a lovely building to house a museum."

"*N'est-ce pas*? / Isn't it charming? The interior is even more so, with a courtyard in the center, formal gardens and vaulted passageways. This site was once a Carmelite convent. Shall we enter?"

I dropped onto the bench, my knees knocking. "Before we do, I need to confess to you who I am."

She sat back down. "Who you are? What do you mean?"

"I *am* Amy Lynch. And I *have* studied archaeology. I *did* come here to volunteer at the dig. The point is how I came to be here. How I heard about the dig. I work for the insurance company which is covering the dig."

"*Je vois* / I see." She sat up straight, eyes wide. "Tell me more."

"I'm a claims investigator. I learned at the office that we would be insuring the dig and became intrigued. So here I am. I intended for this to be a vacation. Toussaint's death has changed my situation."

"So you are now investigating Michel's death?"

"Yes. And the vandalism at the office and the World War II site as well." No point in telling her my inquiries were unofficial so far.

Marie sighed. "I had not thought about the insurance. Too many other pressing matters. Anyway, filing a claim is the responsibility of the Ministry. I will see to it that they do so."

"I realize I should have spoken up sooner."

"With all the goings-on, you had little chance. I was too busy burying myself in my work to spend any time with you."

Relief surged from my pores. "May I ask you a few questions?"

"*Bien sûr.* / Of course. What would you like to know?"

"Do you have any thoughts concerning Toussaint's death? Or the vandalism?"

"*Hélas, non.* / Sadly, no. I only know that his death is a tragedy. As for the vandalism, you best speak with Claude. He can provide you with any information you require."

"Do you know why Toussaint returned to the dig site Sunday evening? When I spoke with him on Sunday, he told me he'd be away for a few days."

"Away from the site, *oui*, but not so far that he couldn't return if he wished."

This was an angle I hadn't considered.

"Michel told me of your meeting on Sunday," Marie continued. "You were fortunate to meet him before..." Her voice trailed off for a moment, then she added, "You made a most favorable impression on him, *vous savez*/ you know. He was looking forward to working with you."

"When did he tell you that?"

"Sunday afternoon, just after he left the dig."

"So the appointment he dashed off to in such a hurry was with you?" *Interesting.*

"*Mais oui.*"

An odd look crossed her face.

"But he saw you here every day. Why rush to meet with you on a Sunday?" I knew the question was nosy. I asked it anyway.

"Just some business we had to discuss, before he left for his business trip on Monday. I was to be in charge during his absence." She stared at her hands. "You must not concern yourself with this business. It was nothing of interest to anyone except ourselves."

Must be business that was none of mine. Were Marie and Michel Toussaint involved in some nefarious enterprise? Or was I over-reacting? I thought not.

Time to move on. "I am curious about the fallen beam."

"What do you mean?"

"I have a hard time believing it came loose from the side supports. Why would anyone install a beam over a deep pit and not take pains to ensure that it was safe?"

"I assure you great pains were indeed taken. The supports were checked regularly to verify their stability. I am unable to explain what happened. Perhaps the surrounding ground became loosened from the rain last week."

Or perhaps not. "What can you tell me about Toussaint's state of mind lately? Was he under a lot of stress?"

Marie's smile returned. "In our business, *mon amie*, one is constantly stressed, and overworked. One always encounters problems to address in the eternal struggle between the great minds of the scientists and the petty regulations of the bureaucrats. But if you are thinking Michel killed himself, you are quite mistaken. Such a thing would be unthinkable." Her voice rose as she said this.

"Unthinkable to you, yes. At least one person seems to feel otherwise."

"And who would that person be, *s'il vous plaît*?"

"I believe it was Solange."

"Solange. I should have known." Marie laughed. "The woman has a personal vendetta against Michel."

"A vendetta?"

"She and Michel were lovers. A most incommodious situation at the worksite, *vous savez* / you know. When Michel chose to end the affair, Solange became bitter."

That didn't surprise me. And it helped to identify the problems with 'other things' Solange had mentioned. "I heard talk about an item which was found last Friday, some kind of a note that Claude unearthed. What do you know about that?"

Marie turned her head away. "I regret, *mon amie*, I cannot say. Now, shall we visit the musée?"

She was hiding something from me. I hoped it was nothing untoward. Marie was a likeable woman. I'd hate to see her mixed up in anything heinous.

"What will you tell the others about me? Can I still work at the dig, at least part-time?"

"*Mon amie*, Amy," Marie laughed. "You are most welcome to do your job and to dig when you can, although I believe the investigation must take priority. And I will not tell the others about your investigation, at least not for now."

# Chapter 12

Our visit to the museum was fascinating, and all too brief. Marie was an excellent docent, explaining the artifacts on display from the dig. A large glass case contained ancient buttons, needles and thimbles, all fashioned out of bone, a set of bone dice, a pair of leather shoes—feet must have been much smaller back then. An area labeled "*L'Artisinat*" displayed pottery of every size, shape and description, most of it with a piece or two missing.

"Pottery is my passion," Marie said. "Reassembling the dishes, vases and bowls. They are seldom retrieved in one piece, *vous savez* / you know. After many years, the work becomes like a child's puzzle, a challenge, yet a pleasure." She consulted her watch. "And now I fear we must cut our visit short. I have obligations to fulfill and meetings to attend. A busy afternoon."

I followed her, dragging my feet. "Are you going back to the rue de Strasbourg?"

"*Oui*."

"Would you mind if I walk with you? I'm hoping to speak with Claude about the damage to his dig-site and his office."

Marie laughed. "There I wish you luck. But of course, accompany me to the office. I shall be happy for your company."

As we made our way up the street, I asked, "Have you been working a long time as an archaeologist?"

"I started shortly before World War II. I had just arrived in Paris as a bride from my home in St. Raphael, on the *Côte d'Azur*. Within a few months, my husband was called to serve in the army. I found myself in need of something to occupy my time. A position became available at the university. My studies qualified me for the post. *Naturellement*, the work was interrupted by the war."

"Is your husband an archaeologist as well?"

"*Hélas*, Amy, he was. My Jean perished during the war."

"How awful for you. Losing him so young must have been very difficult."

Marie's eyes clouded over. "*Difficile, oui*, but not for such reasons as you would think. Jean survived in battle and returned to Paris at the time of the Occupation, only to be sent to Germany as part of a forced labor conscription."

"Good Lord. I had no idea the Germans did that sort of thing." I should have paid more attention in history class.

"Sadly, *oui*. It was an effort by the Germans to free up more of their men of fighting age by replacing factory workers with Frenchmen. Sadly, many fine men so conscripted did not return, my Jean among them. My work provided me with a cause after Jean's death, a reason to continue. I did it for him."

"Life must have been hard for you during the German Occupation."

"It could have been so," Marie said in a near-whisper. "I busied myself with activities far more important than the work I do now. Today I preserve relics of the past. Back then, I worked to preserve life. As did we all."

I stopped short in the middle of the sidewalk. "I beg your pardon?"

"The Résistance, Amy, the underground. I joined them after my Jean was taken away."

"When I think of the Résistance, I picture men hiding in the woods, fighting a guerilla war."

"The men of which you speak were the Maquis. They did indeed hide in the woods and conduct a guerilla war. But many women were involved as well, in other important jobs. They ran the printing presses which produced our literature, hid people awaiting the opportunity to escape, distributed newsletters, carried messages. At first, I worked mainly to help refugees from other occupied countries, providing them with shelter, healing their wounds, eventually getting them out of France. We helped hundreds to escape. Most of them were Jews, but others as well—British soldiers, gypsies, political refugees."

"You operated a safe house? That must have been awfully dangerous."

"*Ah oui* / Indeed it was. For a time, I led a double life, working by day for a professor of archaeology at the University, facing the Germans on a regular basis while sheltering their enemies in my apartment. But the only true danger to me was myself."

"I don't understand."

"The key to successful duplicity," Marie said, "is not to give oneself away. In my case, that meant learning to behave in a natural manner, not allowing my loathing for the Germans to show. Had I displayed the least hostility toward them, I would have become suspect. It was with great distaste that I played the part of the willing victim, accepting the occupying forces without a fight. This hypocrisy was necessary to protect the lives of others until we were able to smuggle them out of France and to safety."

This was getting more intriguing by the minute. "How did you do that?"

"It was not so difficult for me. My brother, Alain, was living in St. Raphael, on the *Côte d'Azur*. He worked closely with Girard, the leader of the underground movement in the south. I was granted a permit to visit my brother, ostensibly on University business. I travelled at irregular intervals. The train service was undependable, yet I did my best. While there, I obtained forged passports from Alain and smuggled them back to Paris. These documents allowed many to escape."

"It must have been terrifying, thinking of what could happen if you'd been caught." I shuddered at the thought.

Marie smiled. "There were subtle tricks I employed to ensure my safety."

"Like what?"

"Like deliberately seating myself in the same compartment as German officers in the train. Conversing with them as if it were the most natural thing in the world. I was assumed to be a collaborator, therefore not bothered by officials checking identity cards or travel permits. As distasteful as this ruse was, it usually worked quite well."

"Usually?" I held my breath.

"One evening, when returning from St. Raphael, the train was boarded by the Gestapo. Unlike my previous trips, despite my apparent friendliness with our invaders, they chose to search me. A terrifying experience. Looking back, I believe they were looking specifically for me. They located the forged passports at once. I was arrested."

"How awful. Did they harm you?"

"I was questioned rather forcibly."

I gasped. "They tortured you?"

"*Oui et non*. They broke all my fingers during the interrogation. The more frightening and painful methods were never employed on me. I do not know why."

I struggled not to stare at her hands. "What a horrible experience for you."

"*Ah, oui*, they may have broken my bones, but never my spirit. Never during those dreadful months of imprisonment. To this day, I do not know where I found such strength. I survived the cold, the near starvation, the brutal interrogations, the loneliness, the boredom. I feared I would lose my mind. They tried to trick me as well, placing spies in my cell disguised as fellow prisoners. I was threatened with deportation to a German labor camp. That is to say, a camp of extermination. The Allies arrived in Paris before this could occur. But through all of this, I never once betrayed the others."

"The others?"

"Gérard, Henri, Jean-Paul. The others in my group. Chantal, Dominique, Katya, Claude. We were great friends. In those days, one knew only those with whom one worked directly. Knowledge was a dangerous commodity. The more Résistance workers one knew, the more one might betray under questioning. We worked in small groups, worked together for a great and noble cause."

Marie smiled softly, a faraway look on her face. "I am pleased to inform you that nearly three quarters of France's 120,000 Jews were saved. My friends and I played some small part in this effort."

"Small part? What you did was amazing. You should be proud."

She brushed off my compliment. "Seldom in life does one find the friendship, the caring, the singleness of purpose that those times held for us. I do not miss the fear, or the sorrow when we were not successful and people died as a result. But the experience taught me to savor each day with great joy, to rejoice in the freedom from fear which I now enjoy."

We arrived at the office as she concluded her story. "And now, I must bid you farewell. I have much business requiring my attention. You should find Claude in his office, the back room on the left. Again, I wish you luck with him."

# Chapter 13

Claude sat at a beat-up wooden desk littered with photos which he studied with a magnifying glass. He didn't react to my knock, didn't look up when I entered the room.

"Excuse me." I approached the desk.

Claude raised his eyes, scowled, then returned to his work.

"I'm sorry to disturb you, but I need to ask you a few questions."

His sour expression was not encouraging.

"*Comment*? / What?" he growled. "What kinds of questions? Who are you anyway?"

I looked him straight in the eye and took a deep breath. "My name is Amy Lynch. I'm an investigator for the company insuring this dig. I came to France for a vacation, to work as a volunteer digger. With Michel Toussaint's death and the other recent incidents, I am now back at work in my investigative capacity. I need information on the break-in at your office and the vandalism to the World War II site."

Claude scowled again. "Insurance, *hein*? As if that would help us now. Michel Toussaint is dead. My site is in ruins. A check from you won't change that, *vous savez*. What is done is done. Now go away. There is important work to do. I am the person best qualified to do it. I have no time to waste answering useless questions. *S'il vous plaît*, leave me in peace."

This wasn't going to be easy. Maybe a little ego massage would break through his crusty exterior. When all else fails, try flattery. "What are you working on here? It looks fascinating. I've always been intrigued by World War II. Are these photos from that dig site?"

He put down his magnifying glass. "Correct. I'm studying the photographs and diagrams we made last Friday. Our custom is to end each week with extensive documentation. Then those of us who are so inclined, who take our work seriously, may use the weekend to study what has been done."

"A sound practice," I told him. "And it may be helpful to me."

"*Comment*? / What do you mean?" He raised his bushy gray eyebrows.

Now was my big chance. I didn't want to blow it. Time to talk to him like a trained archaeologist, appeal to his professional pride. "I was hoping to compare the condition of this site prior to the vandalism incident to what it is now. To see what actual damage was done. Or if anything has been taken."

He almost smiled. "You may not be so dumb after all. That's what I was doing when you disturbed me. I am attempting to determine what was at the site last week that isn't there now."

Progress at last! "What have you found?"

"Nothing yet." Claude picked up the magnifying glass and resumed his study.

"May I look at those with you?"

"If you must, but be quick about it. I am a busy man." He leaned across the table, placing the group of photos where we both could examine them. Holding his magnifying glass over the first, he said, "Here you see the site as it was last Friday. We had just completed removing the rubble from the demolished building."

"The house destroyed by the bomb?"

Claude's scowl almost disappeared. "You know about that, *hein*? There was a bomb, toward the end of the Occupation. The building was partially destroyed, but never demolished. For years, squatters lived in the undamaged portion. We only recently received permission to dismantle the building and explore the site."

"When was the demolition completed?"

"Thursday morning." He pushed two photos toward me. "These are the remains of the building as we found them. Then this photo shows the site with the structure completely razed. My next step was to remove the debris. *Naturellement* after a thorough examination."

"Did you find anything of interest?"

The magnifying glass slipped from his fingers. He fumbled to retrieve it without diverting his eyes from the photos. "*Pardon* / What did you say? I fear I became distracted."

"By what?"

"Something in these two photos I had not noticed earlier. *Regardez ici.* / Look here. These two photos were taken of the same area and from the same angle, this one Friday afternoon, the other Tuesday morning. There are differences. Small, subtle, but differences nevertheless."

I took the magnifying glass and examined the photos, anxious to see what he meant. "Here, the ground appears to have been dusted clean. In the later photo, there are now rocks and debris in the same spot."

"Correct. What else do you see? Or not see?"

"Can't you just tell me? It would take less time."

He threw his hands up. "R*egardez bien.* / Look closely. Here, on Friday, you see this urn. A simple piece of pottery, about

75 centimeters high, overturned and lying by the side of what was once a wall. On Tuesday …"

"The urn is gone. No, Wait. It's still there, only now it's in pieces."

"And you know this how?" he prodded me.

I picked up a pencil to use as a pointer. "Look at this debris. See the marking on it. Now look at the urn. The patterns are the same. Somebody went out of his way to smash the urn."

Claude gave me a thumbs-up. "*Bravo, Mademoiselle*. You have a good eye."

Finally I had something to work with. Not much, but it was a start. "Why would someone need to break this urn?" I did a quick calculation in my head. 75 centimeters was around 2 ½ feet. "It was certainly tall. Was it very valuable? Or special in some way?"

"*Non*, it was quite ordinary. A simple piece of pottery, large, *oui*, but neither old nor expensive." He closed his eyes for a moment. "When we began work on this site, the urn was already damaged, lying on its side."

"Is that significant?"

He shrugged. "There was also a paper in it."

"What sort of paper?"

"Nothing of any importance. Just an old envelope we found inside the urn, crumpled and dirty. It contained a small paper covered with scribbling on it. No language one would recognize. Nonsense. Recent trash, no doubt."

"What became of this paper?"

"Michel took it. On Friday. He hoped to make sense of it. As if he did not trust my judgment. I told him it was trash. He thought otherwise. This was his way of asserting his so-called authority over me. Such a fool, he was, an incompetent scientist."

Something clicked in my memory. "Is this the 'find' I heard people discussing? The one that had Toussaint so excited on Friday?"

"It was found on Friday. That Michel became excited, I cannot say. I can tell you he was of questionable judgment, making much of very little, while often overlooking that which was truly important. Procedures will change once I am put in charge."

I made a mental note of the hostility in this last remark. "What became of this paper?"

"Despite my conviction that it was worthless, I followed standard procedure, making two copies for my files. I gave the original to Michel and returned to my work."

"Do you still have those copies?"

"*Mais oui*."

"May I see them?"

"If you wish." He led me into a small room filled to overflowing with what looked like junk—stones of various sizes, boxes containing unidentifiable small items, all willy-nilly atop old wooden tables.

"Is this where you store your artifacts?"

He nodded. Picking up a small tin box, he shuffled through its contents. "*Voilà*! Here it is. You see, nothing but scribbles and nonsense." He handed me one copy.

I studied it for a moment and was tempted to agree with him. Yet something about this note had caused a stir. "Could I have a copy of this for my report?"

"I suppose."

"May I also make copies of the photos on your desk?"

"If you wish. But I do not understand how they may be of help to you."

"Just being thorough," I lied. Claude had to be missing something. And I intended to find it. "Do you have a copy machine?"

He walked toward an adjoining room. "In here. Let us hope it is functioning today. The machine is old, well-used and somewhat temperamental."

I followed him into the tiny room. Luck was with us; the copier did its job. I copied both the note and the photos, making one set for myself and one for Béchard. "I have just a few more questions for you. Then I'll be on my way. I'm sure you're eager to return to your work."

"I am not sure what else I can tell you."

"What do you think about Toussaint's death?"

He responded immediately, "A tragic accident."

"You sound quite certain."

"What else could it be? You are not hinting at suicide?"

"I don't know," I told him.

"I do." He slammed his fist on the desk. "I knew Michel well. Never would he consider such a thing. His sense of self-importance would not permit it."

"Did you see Toussaint over the weekend?"

"Why should I wish to do such a thing?"

"Or speak with him?"

"*Non.*"

"What about on Monday?"

"*Non,* and *non* again. I can be of no further assistance to you, *Mademoiselle*."

I was being dismissed. It didn't matter. I'd run out of questions. "Thank you for your time. You have been very helpful. I'll see myself out."

He sat down and resumed his work.

I left with more than I had come with. The urn and the note were a start, clues of some sort, despite what Claude thought. I'd figure it out eventually.

# Chapter 14

# Judas

Judas tossed and turned, unable to sleep. The old fears had resurfaced, taken control. They were ruining the life he had worked so hard to achieve, the life he had killed to attain. He couldn't let that happen. He had to regain control.

Who could put it all together as Moreau had done? With that damn note out there, anything could happen. He searched his past for anyone who might be a threat.

Philippe told him Marie gave Moreau the note. Why Marie? Such a lovely woman. He remembered how she was, young, vibrant, dedicated to a cause. She was the only one of them who had a brain. Now she had the note. How could she be working at the very dig-site where the note had been unearthed? Fate should not be that cruel. Hadn't he suffered enough?

Marie could be a problem. She could put it all together. Philippe needed to get to her before she had a chance to figure things out, and to destroy him. He needed to learn everything she knew, everything she had done, everybody to whom she had given a copy of the note. Then she had to be silenced.

He clenched his fists and hoped Philippe would get it right this time.

# Chapter 15

I telephoned Béchard from the *pension* to ask if the police and coroner's reports were ready. They were. We agreed to meet at the Café Procope for a cocktail and an exchange of information, as per our deal.

I spent the remainder of the afternoon taking care of some errands: a trip to American Express to fax my initial claim report to Nancy, then to an ATM, then a *pharmacie* for a few necessities.

I arrived at the Café Procope promptly at 5:00. Béchard was waiting at the door.

"Why did you select this café?" he asked.

"It's a short walk from my *pension.* And I thought it would be nice to see something of the real Paris. The guide books all recommend it. This place is quite well-known."

"Well-known, *oui*, primarily for its history. Look here." He pointed to a marble plaque on the outside wall. "This sums it up nicely."

I read aloud. "The oldest café in the world…frequented by Voltaire, Benjamin Franklin, Robespierre, Napoleon, Victor Hugo…quite a history."

"*Ah, oui,*" Béchard said. "For more than two centuries, this was the meeting place for anybody who was anybody in the world of art, literature or politics, as well as for those who wished to become somebody. In our time, it is mostly a tourist attraction, no longer a gathering place for the locals. And it is expensive, a by-product of its notoriety."

"I'm sure it's worth the price."

We entered the café and sat in a small area in the foyer set apart by a black and white checkered marble floor. I chose a seat with a view of the dining room. Already the Procope was all I had hoped for—exactly what I always pictured Paris to be.

Béchard ordered kir cocktails for both of us. I looked around the room. In a doorway, in large black, faded letters, I read the names of Danton, Marat, Bonaparte, Robespierre—all important figures of the French Revolution. My eyes wandered to a glass display case containing old books and a hat. "That hat looks like something Napoleon would have worn."

"It was." Béchard pointed to the write-up on the back of his menu. "Napoleon left it here as a pledge on his bill. As the hat is still here, one can assume that the bill was never paid."

The waiter arrived with our drinks. We both sipped silently for a moment. Delicious.

Béchard reached into his pocket and handed me a thick envelope. Inside were several typed pages, all very official looking. "These are copies. You may keep them."

"Thanks. You can't imagine how much these will help me." I began to read the documents, then stopped and looked up at Béchard. "These are in French."

"*Naturellement*. This is a problem?"

"Not exactly. I'll just have to translate them before sending them to my office."

"An easy task for you. Your French is excellent. And your accent is thoroughly charming." He added this comment with a hint of a smile.

"But this is technical language. My French is more conversational. I hope I can do it justice." I continued to study the documents while Béchard summoned the waiter and ordered more drinks.

"This makes no sense," I announced after a few moments. "This report says the side supports at the deep pit appeared to be recently installed, and the supposed erosion was inconsistent with the general condition of the ground around the pit. The beam should not have come loose."

"I know. May I suggest you turn your attention to the report of the medical examiner?"

"Is there a surprise here as well?" I read on. "Son of a bitch! Will you look at this!"

"I have already looked."

I read aloud from the report. "Death occurred at approximately 3:00 A.M.... The majority of the contusions on the body are the result of a fall, but they appear to have occurred after death...Cause of death: severe blow to the back of the head." I struggled to lower my voice. "Toussaint didn't kill himself. It wasn't an accident. He was murdered."

"*Hélas, oui.*"

I studied his face, wondering if he was disturbed by this or pleased the case had become more interesting. Hard to tell. "Who do you think did it?"

"That is what we must now discover. Have you any suspicions from what you have heard at the dig? The people I have interviewed so far—André, Georges and Pierre—have been pleasant but unhelpful. Either they know nothing or they prefer not to share their thoughts with the police. Is there anybody you feel might have a motive?"

"Good question. Marie acted strangely today, but that doesn't mean she killed him. Besides, she's too old, too frail, too short."

"Other thoughts?"

"Claude disliked Toussaint. But that's too obvious. If he had killed him he wouldn't be so vocal about his feelings. He acts more like an old crank than a killer."

"How does a killer act?"

I shrugged. "Then there's Solange."

"Another archaeologist?"

"Right."

"How does she figure in?"

"According to Marie, Solange and Toussaint were lovers. She was unhappy when he ended the affair. That could be a motive."

"It could. However, one must exercise caution at all times and thoroughly investigate all possibilities before drawing any conclusions."

I sipped my drink and pondered the possibilities. Béchard was right. We had a lot of work ahead of us.

Béchard broke the silence. "How did you spend your day? Was your meeting with Marie Duprès informative?"

"She's an amazing woman. I heard about the war and her experiences in the Résistance. She's a hero." I repeated Marie's story.

Béchard listened, nodding his head. "Indeed?"

"Doesn't that amaze you?"

"Impress, perhaps, amaze, *non.* In France, nearly everybody of a certain age has a story from the war. Some are of more interest than others. Marie's is beyond the usual. But what of Toussaint's death? Was she able to provide any information? I have not yet spoken with her myself, as she has so far successfully resisted my attempts to interview her."

"She spoke as if Toussaint's death was an accident."

"You doubt her sincerity?"

"I'm skeptical, professionally speaking. Marie is an intelligent woman. She knows the insurance wouldn't pay in a case of suicide."

Béchard remained silent. His expression did nothing to give away his thoughts.

I continued. "There's something else, but I can't quite put my finger on it."

"Put your finger on it?"

"An American expression," I laughed, "meaning I can't determine exactly what it is. I'm not even sure I can explain it to you. Just a feeling I have."

"A feeling about what?"

"That's there's something more, something Marie is not telling me. For one thing, she met with Toussaint on Sunday afternoon. She was very vague about why, practically told me it was none of my business."

"Why should this not be so?"

"Because she was so open and friendly the rest of the time. Actually, she got odd one other time as well. When I asked her about the note Claude found on Friday."

"Here you lose me completely."

"Sorry. I thought I had already mentioned that to you." I filled him in on the note. "When I spoke of it to Marie, she shut me out. All she said was 'I cannot say.' Did that mean she didn't know or that she wasn't willing to discuss it? She avoided eye contact when she said this."

"Professional secrets, perhaps?"

"Maybe. Except that later, when I was speaking with the archaeologist Claude, he not only told me about the note, he gave me a copy of it. It's nothing special that I can tell, just an old piece of paper with some writing that doesn't seem to make sense."

"Claude?" Béchard consulted his notebook. "He has not yet been available to meet with me either. He put me off twice before scheduling a meeting for tomorrow."

“That doesn’t surprise me. He’s a cranky old guy.” I reached into my bag for a copy of the note and handed it to Béchard.

He studied it in silence.

“Do you see what I mean? I can’t imagine why Marie would be hesitant to discuss this with me.”

“You mean you are unable to place your finger on it?” He flashed me a full-dimpled grin.

“What do you think about the timing of the vandalism incidents and the death of Toussaint? An odd coincidence, don’t you think?” I asked.

“I am confident we will discover a connection.”

I rifled through my bag again, retrieving the copies of Claude’s photos. I placed them on the tiny table so we could both see them and explained to Béchard what Claude had shown me.

“Interesting,” he said, “I will question Claude at length about it when I see him. I have an appointment with him tomorrow afternoon. I nearly had to threaten the man to convince him to speak with me.”

“Where do we go from here?”

“Back to the dig site. Back over the reports. Back to question people one more time. We need to uncover a motive, a suspect and the instrument with which Toussaint was struck. There remains much to do. And much to learn.”

# Chapter 16

Béchard walked me back to the *pension.* He didn't mention dinner, so I decided our cocktail hour had been a business meeting, not a date. That was OK. Maybe even a relief. We said good night at the door. I was eager to have a quick dinner, then spend the evening translating the police and coroner's reports.

Dinner was just being served in the dining room. I ate in record time, then returned to my room to work on my translations and put together a follow-up report for Nancy. There was something I needed to do first, though, and it was definitely overdue. My conscience and I sat on the bed and dialed Pete's cell. I should have tried harder to reach him, for better or for worse.

"Ames! Hello! I was just thinking about you. All good thoughts. And planning to give you a call this evening."

Pete was nothing if not enthusiastic.

"How are you?" I asked.

"Fine."

He sounded fine. Maybe my concerns about him, us, were all in my mind. "It's so good to hear your voice, Pete. I miss you." Realizing how much I meant it, I felt a twinge of guilt that I hadn't tried harder to reach him before. "Sorry I didn't get to speak with you sooner. Things have been a little crazy here."

"Peggy told me."

"And she told me you stopped by to see Sam."

"Yes, I've been walking with him every afternoon. I figure if I'm going to get some exercise anyway, I might as well do it with my buddy Sam. The mutt is good company."

"Yes, he's a wonderful listener. Thanks for visiting him. I'm sure he loves seeing you."

"Yeah, but I can tell he misses you. So, according to Peggy, you've been busy over there. Not much of a vacation."

I sighed. "Too true. The past few days have been interesting and then some."

"Did you find out how that archaeologist died?"

"He was murdered." I shuddered as I spoke the words.

"Geez, Ames, that's awful."

I filled him in on everything that had happened to date.

"Between the murder at the dig and the major brouhaha you created at the office, your life is certainly interesting these days. That's what I love about you, Ames. You're never dull."

"How did you know about my problems at work?"

"From Peggy. She says even Old Man Fisher is furious with you."

"So they tell me, though I can't imagine why he even cares. Up until now, the man barely acknowledged my existence. I don't get it."

"I wish I could be there to comfort you and help you," he said. "I enjoyed working on that case in Key West with you. And it sounds like you've got your hands full."

"That's for sure."

Did he want to fly over to help me? Did I want him to? How would his being in Paris affect my relationship with Béchard? Our association was officially all work, but the guy was adorable. And he seemed interested in me. I gulped. Better not to pursue that thought. "I have to get back to work now, translating some documents for the file."

"I understand. Glad you called. I love you."

"Love you too, Pete. I'll call again soon." I ended the call then realized that I hadn't asked him how his court case was progressing. Not good. I'd make it a point to ask next time. Right now, I needed to get to work.

I grabbed my French-English dictionary. I'd need it for the metric conversion tables. Tossing the book onto the bed along with a pad of paper, a pen and the reports, I sat cross-legged to begin what I expected to be a tedious task.

Translating wasn't as difficult as I feared. The technical terms turned out to be remarkably similar to their English counterparts. Shortly after midnight, the job was complete. I headed for the shower to wash away the events of the day.

As I returned to my room, I nearly collided with Madame Hulot. Tonight she was wearing an ankle-length skirt in bright pink and green with a pink polka-dot blouse. The outfit set off both her rotund figure and her flaming red hair. She jumped when she saw me.

"Sorry, Madame," I said. "I didn't mean to startle you."

"*Ah, non, excusez-moi*, Amy. I was not paying attention. I was about to leave a message on your door." She handed me a slip of paper. "From a charming lady named Marie Duprès. She said it was most important."

I struggled to read the handwritten message in the dim hallway light. Marie needed to speak with me as soon as possible on an urgent matter. Could I please meet her at the dig office the next morning? She would be there no later than 8:00.

"She didn't leave a number where I could reach her?"

Madame Hulot shook her head.

*How urgent could her dilemma be if she didn't need a call back tonight?*

Once in my room, I reread Marie's note and planned my morning. If I met her at the dig at 8:00, that would delay faxing these papers to Nancy. Though with the time difference between Paris and Boston, I should be able to meet with Marie and still send the fax before the office opened in Boston.

My eyes stung from overwork in less-than-adequate light, my head was reeling from too little sleep and one cocktail too many. I lay back and thought about my conversations of the day—with Marie, with Claude, with Béchard. None of it seemed real. Toussaint had been murdered. Marie was a hero from the Résistance. Marie was hiding something. Then there was Claude. Was he just plain surly, or was there something more? Most of all, what about Pete? Were we meant to be? After he nearly died in Key West last spring, I was convinced we were. Then why was I so attracted to Béchard?

# Chapter 17

Waking early from an uncomfortable sleep, I downed a quick cup of coffee and dashed to the Métro, curious to learn what Marie wanted, or needed. Exiting the station, I hurried along to the rue de Strasbourg. It was a little after 7:45. The office was unlocked.

"*Qui est là*?" Marie called out. "Who is there?"

"*C'est moi*, Amy Lynch."

Marie's small form appeared at the top of the stairs. Somehow, today she looked smaller, less full of life. "I am happy you have come. Please join me up here so we may speak privately."

I climbed the narrow stairs and followed Marie into her office, taking a seat opposite her desk. "I got your message. Sorry I missed your call last night. If you had left a number, I would have called you back."

"*Hélas*, I was so agitated, I did not think to do so."

She still appeared to be agitated.

"What can I do for you?" I asked.

"I apologize for involving you in problems which are not yours." Marie's voice was unsteady. Tears streamed down her cheeks. She sobbed loudly.

I searched my bag for a notebook and pen, mostly to give her time to cry.

She took a deep breath and dried her eyes. “I beg your pardon. In my younger days, fear meant little to me. At this age I do not cope with it as well. I find myself terrified at the moment, and unsure how to proceed. Or where to turn. Or who to trust.”

“What terrifies you so?”

“I am in fear for my life.” Her voice quivered.

“Shouldn’t you be speaking with the police?”

Marie sighed. “That would perhaps be wise. However, I am reluctant to do so. During the Occupation, one learned not to trust the police, or anybody in authority. Involvement with the police usually ended in disaster, or treachery, or accusations—or worse.”

“I understand. Still, Inspector Béchard, who’s investigating Michel Toussaint’s death, is not at all intimidating. Once you’ve met him, you’ll feel you can trust him. But I’m happy to help you if I can.”

“Sometimes one finds it easier to confide in a stranger. I learned to read people well during my days in the Résistance. I believe you to be a kind person. My instincts tell me I can trust you.”

“Please tell me what has happened.”

Slowly, quietly, almost as if talking to herself, Marie began her story. “My dilemma started last Friday, with Claude working on the World War II site. He uncovered something which has been the cause of many terrible things.”

“You mean that note with the strange writing on it?”

Marie’s eyes grew wide. “You know of this note?”

“Claude showed it to me yesterday. He didn’t attach any importance to it.”

Marie was visibly shaken by this. “Claude is a fool.”

“He gave me a copy. For my report.”

"Your report, *bien sûr* / of course. I suppose it should be included there."

"But what is this note?"

"It is a coded message from the time of the Occupation. A message from a traitor. "

*Good lord. Was I hearing correctly?* "How do you know that?"

"In the Résistance, we all used codes to some extent. A necessary part of our work. While I was never expert at this, I am able to recognize an encoded document."

"Were you able to decipher it?"

"*Hélas*, non. Not yet. I have been struggling with it since Friday and am making slow progress. Right now, I must tell you what took place last Friday after the note was found."

I moved forward in my chair.

"When Claude brought the paper to Michel, he came immediately to me with it. We made several copies with which to work, wrapped the original in plastic to preserve it and locked it away. Michel was most eager to discover its meaning. I offered to speak with some friends from the old days who were expert in codes."

She blinked away the moisture in her eyes. "I contacted a colleague from the Résistance, named Richard Moreau. He was willing and able to help. I gave Michel his name and telephone number. Moreau was expecting to hear from Michel."

"Did Toussaint contact Moreau?"

"He went to Moreau's home Saturday evening. This I know because Moreau telephoned me Sunday morning. Michel gave him a copy of the message. Moreau succeeded in decoding it. And this, I fear, has cost him his life. Such a foolish man he was."

"Moreau is dead?"

"Sadly, *oui*."

"But how? What happened?"

"How he died is unclear. I found his body when I went to his apartment Sunday evening."

"What did you do?"

"I called the police at once, even though I knew it was too late. The Medical Examiner pronounced him dead, saying Moreau was old; his heart simply gave out." She paused and gave a little shudder. "I dispute the Medical Examiner's finding. I believe Moreau was murdered."

"What makes you say this?" I asked, horrified at the idea.

"I knew the man well for many years, and saw him often. He was in excellent health."

Marie's assessment of Moreau's health didn't exactly point to murder. "Was there anything else that made you suspect foul play?"

Marie let out a ragged sigh. "There is something more. When I spoke with Moreau earlier Sunday, he told me much of what he had decoded, although not all. What he said filled my heart with hatred and with fear."

I sat at attention, almost afraid of what she might tell me next.

"During the war," Marie continued, "we had begun to suspect a traitor in our midst. Things occurred which could have no other explanation."

"What kind of things?"

"Well-planned operations went wrong for no apparent reason. People we were helping to escape were captured, by means we never could discover. Over time, we came to realize that such events were possible only if one of our own was supplying the Germans with information. It is a terrible thing to work with people in a vital cause only to learn that one among you cannot be trusted."

"What happened?" And how did this relate to the late Moreau and the coded message?

"We suspected a member of our group named Antoine. Whether he was guilty or not we shall never know. I am ashamed to say we executed him. Shot him in the head without providing him with the opportunity to defend himself. To this day, his image haunts me. The horror on his face as he died still fills me with guilt."

My jaw dropped.

"The incidents stopped for a while, then began again. The traitor was still among us. We never discovered who it was. There were people we suspected, but never any proof. Until now."

"The note?"

"*Oui*. Moreau called to tell me he had decoded it. While he told me little of what the note actually said, he was convinced it identified the traitor in our group. Moreau was both angry and excited. It frightened me."

I wrote furiously as Marie spoke, not wishing to miss a word. "And who was it?"

"*Hélas*, I do not know. He would not speak of it on the telephone, for fear of being overheard. He was also convinced he had been followed. I was to go to his apartment that evening to learn the identity of the traitor. I arrived too late. I now believe Moreau was murdered, just as Michel was."

I dropped my pen and notebook onto the floor. "You knew all along Toussaint's death wasn't an accident?"

"*Oui*. I beg you to forgive me for keeping this from you. I did so out of fear."

"How did you know?"

"A small thing. Something only an old friend would know. Michel telephoned me Sunday evening as I was leaving to visit Moreau. I was surprised to hear from him, as we had met together just a few hours earlier. He was calling to say he had heard from Moreau. Then he said something strange before hanging up."

"What did he say?"

"That Moreau's son had asked to meet with him to get a copy of the note. The son said Moreau was ill and unable to go himself. But he wanted to begin decoding as soon as possible."

"Why was this strange?"

"Moreau had no son. Sadly, Michel was off the phone before I could tell him this. Now I feel I am responsible for his death."

"You think this alleged son killed Toussaint? And Moreau as well?"

"It would appear so, I regret to say."

I digested this information. "How did this note end up at Claude's dig site?"

"One can only speculate. My belief is that it was left there deliberately. To be retrieved later by the Germans."

"You mean the urn was a dead drop?"

Marie stared at me. "You are familiar with the term?"

"I read a lot of spy novels."

"You are correct. I believe the urn was the traitor's dead drop. And in this case, the message was never picked up."

"Until last week. When Claude found it in the broken urn."

"The fact that I am working on the dig where this note was discovered confirms my belief in fate. Had it fallen into different hands, this message would most likely have been dismissed as nonsense, probably discarded. I recognized it for what it is."

"Karma," I said.

"Indeed. It was Karma." Marie stared at her gnarled and crooked hands as if willing them not to shake. "There is one other thing Moreau told me Sunday morning. When he identified the traitor, so great was his anger and indignation that he did something completely out-of-character. Where he found the courage, I do not know. Moreau telephoned the traitor. How he located the man after all these years is a mystery to me. Moreau threatened to expose the traitor, and reveal his crimes. If only Moreau had spoken to me first. I would have talked him out of it. I could have saved his life." She began to cry again.

"So you think it was this traitor who called Toussaint? Then killed him?"

"It would appear so. If only Moreau had been less cautious, less paranoid about discussing things over the phone. Then we might know the identity of this monster." She wiped her eyes and fell silent.

I retrieved my notebook from the floor and scanned it. "You said you're afraid for your life. Why? Has something else happened?"

"*Oui*. And that is what convinced me to telephone you"

"What was it?"

"Last night, as I headed home, I was followed."

"Are you sure?"

"*Absolument*. One does not survive in the Résistance without developing certain skills and instincts. I was followed."

"Did you see who it was? Can you describe him?"

Marie shook her head. "I can tell you he was too young to have been one of us. Perhaps thirty or forty. Fairly ordinary looking. And most definitely following me. Not very well, though, or I would not have noticed him so quickly."

"Did he approach you? Try to harm you?"

A mournful smile crossed her lips. "I did not provide him with the opportunity to do so. I am old now, but one remembers tricks, especially those ruses which ensure one's safety. When I became certain he was after me, I reverted to my old training and was able to elude him. Not an easy task. I required an hour of travel around the city before feeling certain my pursuer was no longer with me and I could return home."

"I'm impressed. But I'm not sure what we do from here."

"Nor am I. However, I do not regret my decision to speak with you."

"I understand how you feel about the police. Nevertheless, I think we should tell Béchard about this. For your own protection."

"I will consider doing so. But not today. Perhaps tomorrow, after Michel's funeral."

I cringed at the thought, but forced myself to say," I will be there." I had no choice; it was part of my job.

Marie wrote on a piece of paper and handed it to me. "Here is the location of the funeral, the church of St. Sulpice. At 10:00."

"Béchard may want to come as well. If so, you can meet him and make arrangements to speak with him at length, although I'd prefer you do it today. Do you want me to stay here with you? To keep you company?"

"*Merci.* That is most kind of you. But not necessary. I have things which must be done. I will be fine. I must be brave. I am feeling better now, just knowing you will help me."

"Will you forgive me if I beg off work at the dig today?" And talk to Béchard myself if Marie wasn't willing to do so.

"*Mais oui.*" Marie rose and held out her hand, my cue to leave.

I didn't feel right leaving Marie alone, but I couldn't force myself on her. Besides I could do more to help her by speaking with Béchard—as soon as possible.

# Chapter 18

I practically ran to the Métro station, wanting to speak with Béchard as quickly as possible. If Marie was in danger, he needed to know.

I had my pick of seats on the nearly-empty train. Selecting a spot in the rear of the car, I plopped down to catch my breath and collect my thoughts. Béchard's office was on the Île de la Cité, in the middle of the river. The Métro map indicated I should change trains at Champs-Elysées station, exit at Châtelet and walk from there. That settled, I sat back and closed my eyes, planning my next move.

Then a chill attacked my body like somebody was walking on my grave. Opening my eyes, I noted a man standing by the door and staring at me. His appearance was unremarkable except for a tattoo on his left forearm. A bright red tattoo. He was too far away for me to see what it depicted. Our eyes met for a split second, the look on his face somewhere between creepy and intense.

Willing myself not to shudder, I consulted the Métro map in my lap, more to avoid looking at him than to verify my route. Champs-Elysées was the next stop. Stuffing the map into my shoulder bag, I prepared to exit the car. As soon as the train stopped I hurried past the creep and through the door, never looking back.

Exiting the next train at Châtelet, I headed to the Seine River and the Île de la Cité. I couldn't miss #9, the Préfecture de Police. The building took up two city blocks.

I had been in many police stations in and around Boston in the course of my job. It was no big deal—go in, ask for the reports I needed, maybe interview an officer. This was different. Foreign territory. I hoped the French bureaucracy was less complicated than I had heard.

"*Mademoiselle*?"

I looked up to see a uniformed policeman guarding the door.

"*Pardon, Mademoiselle*, entry is not permitted here."

"I understand that, Officer. I am here on official business. I must see Inspecteur Béchard concerning a case of his." I could sound official, or officious, when I wanted to.

"Your name, *s'il vous plaît*."

"Amy Lynch." I spelled it for him slowly.

He wrote it down, slowly and waived me through the door. "*Attendez ici un moment* / Wait here." The policeman turned and picked up a phone. A minute later he informed me *Inspecteur* Béchard was on his way.

I looked around the station. It was old, as were many buildings in Paris. And absolutely elegant. The ceilings were high, beautifully carved and adorned with an abundance of gilt trim. Obviously not originally built as a police station.

"*Ah bonjour*, Amy." Béchard entered from a hall off to the right. If I read his face correctly, it showed surprise but not displeasure. Once again, he was wearing the suit I had begun to think of as his uniform. The shirt and tie were the ones he had worn the first time I saw him at the dig.

"I'm happy you're available. I need to speak with you."

Béchard smiled. “Let us not stand here discussing business. Please, come to my office.” He led me down a long hallway devoid of furniture or signage, but overflowing with carvings on the walls and paintings on the ceilings. We arrived at a small cluttered room. Béchard entered first, then motioned me to an uncomfortable looking chair. “Would you care for a coffee?”

“No thanks. I’m fine.” I pulled out my notebook, located the pages I needed and looked up at him. “You’re never going to believe this.” I proceeded to relate my incredible conversation with Marie.

Béchard said nothing during my narrative. His pen moved at top speed as he scribbled some notes.

“What do you think?”

“You do indeed provide me with many surprises. This is all quite interesting.”

“And…?”

“And if the story of Marie is to be believed, I may now find myself faced with two murders. That of Toussaint should not be difficult to prove. Someone attempted to make it appear an accident, but the medical examiner’s report refutes this. Moreau is another story. I shall make inquiries into his death.” He paused. “It appears possible the same person may be responsible for both deaths, as well as the vandalism at the dig site and break-in at the office. Marie has provided a plausible motive for these acts. More than that, she has given us a lead to help us identify the guilty party.”

“You mean the traitor?”

“*Mais oui* / But of course. All that remains is to identify this person, then locate him. To prove the charges would be fairly routine, if our assumptions are indeed accurate.”

“You speak as if the task were easy. How do you plan to identify this person, let alone find him?”

“Easy, *non*. Possible, *absolument*.”

"How?"

"First, I get my best people in the reading of codes. Or had you forgotten I have such means at my disposal?"

I hadn't thought about it. "That should help."

"Then I must speak with Marie Duprès as soon as possible."

"Right. Let's call her now and make arrangements. I'm worried about her. If she's right about being followed, then she is in danger. We should get to her right away."

"We?"

"Yes, we. A deal is a deal."

He consulted a telephone directory, then picked up the phone. Ten minutes later, he gave up in frustration. "No answer at the dig office. No answer at Marie's home. They must be the only two telephones in all of Paris which do not have an answering machine. If you will excuse me for a moment, I shall arrange to have men visit both the office and her home and bring her in to speak with me at once."

He stepped out of the room. I used the time to collect my thoughts. When he returned, I told him, "Tomorrow is Toussaint's funeral. I plan to go."

"I shall attend as well. Do you know the location and the time?"

I fished through my shoulder bag for the paper Marie had given me.

He copied the information, then handed it back.

"Do you want me to meet you there?" I asked.

"*Voyons* / let's see. The church of St. Sulpice is not far from your *pension*. I shall call for you there at 9:45. We will walk to the church together. Does this meet with your approval?"

"Sounds good. But I do have a question."

"What is that?"

"A few minutes ago, you said something about if the traitor is indeed the guilty party. What did you mean?"

"I meant, my friend, that while the story which Marie told you is intriguing, one must not discount other possibilities."

"Such as?"

He reread his notes. "Marie may have had other motives in relating this story to you. The story may be untrue, or may be unrelated to the present circumstances. Others at the dig may have had a motive to kill Toussaint. The possibilities are endless, *vous savez*."

"I see. Marie seemed genuinely distressed today. I took it for granted she was telling me the truth." And my gut agreed with me. "I guess you're right." I hesitated, then added, "Before I go, can I ask a favor of you?"

"*Naturellement*. What is it?"

"Do you have a fax machine I could use? I'm happy to pay for it. I have to get this report to my office as fast as I can."

"Did the translation of the documents go well?"

"Better than I expected. I managed to translate everything, put together a decent report and still get some sleep. It's too bad it's hand-written, but I had no choice. It is legible enough."

"I am happy to provide you with the use of our fax machine, at no cost. This is fair in view of the assistance you are providing me. Come. I will take you to the machine."

He led me down another hallway every bit as long as the first, and equally ornate. We arrived at a small room containing a photocopy machine, some machine whose function eluded me and, thank God, the fax. Béchard helped me input the proper international long-distance codes, then we both watched as, one by one, the pages of my report went through the machine on their way to Nancy. Neither of us spoke during the process.

The fax completed and confirmation received, we trekked down the long gilded corridor toward Béchard's office. He hummed tunelessly as we walked.

"I should go now," I said. "I've taken up enough of your time. Thanks for the use of the fax machine."

"It is my pleasure, as always. I thank you for your input into my investigation. It is proving to be most illuminating." Béchard escorted me down the corridor and back to the door where I had entered. He agreed to call me at the *pension* if he succeeded in locating Marie. We both felt their conversation would go better if I were present.

I started out on foot, wondering what to do with the rest of the afternoon.

# Chapter 19

I decided to walk back to the *pension*, slowly. A leisurely stroll would give me a chance to experience Paris. I headed off the Île de la Cité toward the Left Bank.

Heading down a narrow side street, I came upon a small antique shop. In the window was a lovely carved chess set. It appeared to be ivory. As I peered into the glass for a better look, something caught my attention. In the reflection in the glass, a man came to a sudden halt directly across the street. He stood there, gazing in my direction.

He seemed familiar. But that was crazy. How in the world could I see somebody I knew on a little side street in Paris?

Then I saw the red tattoo and gasped. He was the same creepy person who had been watching me in the Métro. The sight of him didn't make me feel warm and fuzzy. I started walking again.

Once across the Seine, I arrived at the bouquinistes stalls. Somewhat akin to a flea market at home—these are small open shops crowded with old postcards, even older books, posters both new and old, maps and everything else you could imagine in the way of printed material, all displayed with no discernible logic.

I stepped into the first stall, keeping a surreptitious eye on my stalker. He loitered on the sidewalk, staring at the river, as if unaware of me.

I browsed for a while, leafing through one book after another, poring over posters, undisturbed by the proprietors. Nobody seemed concerned about making a sale.

After confirming the tattooed stranger was still nearby, I checked out the next stall. It appeared to specialize in books dealing with World War II. I entered to investigate further. Flipping through one volume after another, I looked for references to Paris. In a beat-up yellowed old volume with mold on the binding, I found it: La Résistance Parisienne.

I scanned several pages before coming to a section of old photographs. I read the names of those depicted. And there I found her. The text below a faded old photograph, somewhat out of focus, identified Marie Duprès, Louis Jubon, Jean-Paul Pêcheur and Jean Renoud. Five others were not named. The photograph was blurry, but there was no mistaking Marie. The shape of the face was the same, but mostly it was the eyes, those gorgeous sparkling eyes. Even in black and white I would have known them anywhere.

I studied the others in the photo. They must be the comrades Marie had spoken about. Her fellow Résistance workers and great friends, the ones she had not betrayed, even when imprisoned and tortured. They looked ordinary enough, not my idea of heroes. Go figure.

I shivered, remembering that one of them was also a traitor and had quite probably murdered Toussaint. Perhaps Moreau as well.

There was no question about buying the book. I'd read it in depth after dinner. Maybe gain some insight into Marie Duprès.

Leaving the bouquiniste, I looked for my stalker. He was nowhere in sight. Relieved, I headed in the direction of the *pension,* then remembered I needed to buy some post cards to send home. At the next stall, I found the very thing, modern pictures of Paris: Notre Dame, the Eiffel Tower, the Arc de Triomphe, all the sights my family would expect to see. I selected a dozen of them, then looked for the proprietor to pay for them.

Instead I saw Tattoo, poring through a pile of old manuscripts as if fascinated by them, not seeming to notice me. I took a long, hard look, memorizing his face. Maybe mid-thirties, thin, angular face, small dark eyes, tight little mouth, longish brown hair. Fairly ordinary. Except for the red tattoo. No question in my mind. The man was following me.

Seeing this creep was a good thing. Better to know where he was than to wonder where he might be lurking. I had to get back to the *pension* to call Béchard. He'd know what to do. And I had to get there without my stalker in tow.

I paid for the postcards, stuffed them in my bag and looked up to see my pursuer turn his head away, as if waiting for the light to cross the street. Taking off at a near run, I hurried down the Boulevard St. Michel to the Boulevard St. Germain. This was the most heavily-populated route back. These boulevards were crowded and lively at all hours of the day and night. With luck, I'd lose him. Being short helped. I elbowed my way to the corner of the rue du Four and the Boulevard St. Germain, loitering there until sure he was no longer behind me. Then I speed-walked to the *pension* and the safety of my room, eager to call Béchard.

"Allô, ici Paul Béchard."

"Thank God you're still there!"

"Amy? You sound distressed. Are you all right? Has something happened?"

"I'm fine, but when I left your office, I took a walk along the Seine. There was a man who showed up everywhere I went. He was the same man who was staring at me in the Métro earlier." I described my pursuer in detail.

"Did he approach you?"

"No. He was just always there, pretending not to notice me. It made me nervous." A fact I hated to admit, even to myself. "At first, I thought I was imagining it. Then I recognized the tattoo on his arm. I had noticed it on the Métro. Because it was bright red. I had never seen a completely red tattoo before. I'm positive he was the same man."

"Were you able to judge his age?"

"Probably mid-thirties to early forties."

"How did you manage to lose him?"

"I hurried to the Boulevard St. Michel, to be where there were lots of people. I tried to lose myself in the crowd. It worked."

"You made a wise choice in selecting that route. After the funeral tomorrow, you and I shall attempt to identify this man with the red tattoo. You will visit the station and provide our artist with a description. The tattoo should help to identify him."

After a moment of silence, Béchard added. "Bear in mind that you are investigating not one, but possibly two murders. And that Marie Duprès was followed last night."

"You think it's all connected?"

"It is difficult to be sure. This man could be somebody who finds you attractive and wishes to make your acquaintance. However, it is best to exercise caution. Are you at your *pension* now?"

"Yes."

"I believe it is best for you to remain there, for your own protection and peace of mind. We will discuss this further when I see you in the morning."

"You mean spend the rest of the day in my room? That's a hell of a way to spend my time in Paris."

"While I agree with your sentiment, your safety is the primary issue. Please remain in your room."

"I suppose you're right. I bought some postcards. Writing them will keep me occupied."

"Will you write to Sam?"

I laughed. "Sam can't read. He's a dog."

"*Ah, oui. Eh bien*, I will see you in the morning."

# Chapter 20

I was up before six the next morning, unable to sleep any longer and dreading Toussaint's funeral. The last funeral I'd been to was for my fiancé Danny. For the past few years, I'd managed to avoid all others. When Pete's mother passed away I was out of town on business. And Pete understood when I didn't hurry back. The issue wasn't that I didn't care. I simply couldn't deal with the painful memories. But I couldn't avoid Toussaint's funeral today; this one was business.

I showered and slipped into the one decent dress I had brought with me—a knee-length navy knit from Lands' End. I even wore heels. A funeral was, after all, a formal occasion.

Béchard was wearing a different suit, and no man purse. Today's ensemble was navy blue with a faint stripe, most likely the one he saved for formal occasions. And he looked great in it—almost too much so. With me in my navy dress, we looked pretty good together. Banishing that thought, I chided my libido and asked, "Did your men catch up with Marie yesterday?"

"*Hélas, non*. She was not at her home, nor at her office. We are still unable to contact her by phone at either location. I have men continuing the search for her this morning and hope to have news soon."

"I'm worried about her."

"I am as well. Her absence is most disquieting." He let out a huge sigh. "And so, *mon amie*, have you recovered from your experience of yesterday?"

"Sure have. Can't let a creepy stalker ruin my day." I sounded braver than I felt.

He gestured toward the rue Bonaparte, indicating the direction we would take.

Not used to walking in heels, I stumbled slightly on the sidewalk.

"*Attention*," Béchard said, reaching out to catch me. "Please be careful where you step. It would be most inconvenient if you were to injure yourself."

"You're right. I better watch where I'm going. Not to mention who may be going there with me, invited or not."

"Do not concern yourself. I am here to protect you. I consider that part of our deal."

That worked for me.

He looked at my shoes. "You are taller today."

"Two-inch heels." I lifted a foot to show him, then said, "You'll never believe what I found at a bouquiniste stall yesterday." I described the book on the Résistance Parisienne. "What do you think about that?"

"Quite a coincidence." He stopped and stood facing a large gothic structure in the middle of the square.

"Is this the church? It's beautiful." It was much larger than the churches at home. Two symmetrical bell towers adorned the façade. A group of statues guarded the entrance.

"It must be," Béchard responded.

"You haven't been here before?"

"To the church of St. Sulpice, *non*. Why do you ask?"

"You get to make three wishes."

"I beg your pardon?"

"Each time you visit a church where you've never been before, you get three wishes."

"This is the custom where you live?"

"Yes."

"In that case, I suggest we both wish first to identify Toussaint's killer, then to locate and arrest him. The third wish must be that the man who followed you will be apprehended."

It was hard to tell if he was pulling my leg. He was so serious most of the time. As for me, my first wish was that I'd get over my infatuation with Béchard, since no good could come of it. Secondly, I wished that Pete and I would stop dancing around each other and get it right once and for all. My third wish was for all of Béchard's wishes to come true.

Béchard's voice interrupted my thoughts. "If you do not object, I prefer to enter at once. This will afford us the opportunity to observe the mourners as they arrive." He pulled his cell phone from his jacket pocket, muted the volume and put it back.

I followed him into the church. The interior was old, mostly stone. It was cool, musty and dimly lit. My first surprise was the size of the place—over two football fields wide and God knows how long. Second was the absence of pews. Instead, straight-backed chairs were arranged in rows.

The main altar, two-thirds of the way up the center aisle, was decorated in an amazing amount of gold, with six large candlesticks holding tall white candles. There was a large gold crucifix in the center, as well as a golden pulpit which could be reached only by climbing a small circular stairway. A bit ornate for my tastes, but I grew up in Puritan New England.

Béchard and I stationed ourselves in the rear, to the side of the door. This provided an excellent view of everybody who entered.

André, Pierre and Georges entered together, looking uncomfortable in suits. Solange was alone, dabbing her eyes with a lace handkerchief. Claude was solo as well, his expression less surly than the last time I saw him. The mourners were mostly people in their thirties, many of whom I recognized from the dig. Conspicuously absent was Marie. Or had she slipped in unnoticed by me, surrounded by taller individuals? I hoped that was the case.

I didn't recognize anybody else—probably relatives and friends. A woman in black walked behind the coffin, most likely the widow.

The service was a full mass, complete with haunting organ music and a soloist. Béchard sat very still, his eyes focused on the altar. There were two short eulogies, one by a relative whose relationship I couldn't figure out, the other by a colleague I had never seen at the dig. I fidgeted and fretted about Marie, still hoping to spot her in the crowd, trying not to worry.

The priest descended from the altar to bless the coffin. Several mourners joined him, each sprinkling holy water on the coffin as they passed.

Béchard whispered in my ear. "I wish to exit now. You will join me?"

We stood outside the door, watching and waiting. Neither of us spoke as the priest, then the coffin, and finally the mourners emerged. The church emptied at an appropriately funereal pace. Marie was not among those exiting.

I turned to Béchard. "Please tell me you've seen Marie. I'm very worried."

Béchard shook his head and scanned the crowd.

"*Bonjour*, Amy," a voice behind me said. I turned to see André.

"It was very kind of you to come. This is a most sad occasion, *n'est-ce pas*?" André nodded in Béchard's direction. "We meet again, *Monsieur l'Inspecteur*."

Having no clue as to proper funeral etiquette in France, I said, "There certainly are a lot of people here."

"Michel had many friends. I also see many people from the Ministry."

"I haven't seen Marie yet. Do you know where she is?"

André's face turned ashen. "You haven't heard the news?"

"What do you mean?" This couldn't be good.

"It is tragic." He choked on the words. "Marie is dead. She has been killed."

Béchard let out a low growling noise and reached for his phone. He stepped away from us as he placed a call. The distance didn't help; his angry voice carried back to us and beyond. "Why wasn't I informed sooner?" he shouted, then began digging for details. "When? Where? Send a car for me at once."

He jammed the phone into his pocket and turned to me. "A police car is on its way to pick us up. We must get to Montmartre at once. And later, when I return to the station, heads are going to roll."

The car materialized even as he spoke. We hopped into the back, Béchard with virtual steam coming out of his ears, me a jumbled mass of horror and questions. I stifled a sob.

He gave me a quick pat on the shoulder. "It is sad. But let us not dwell on our own emotions. We must be about our work and discover what has happened—and why I was not informed earlier." He scowled.

It was a few moments before I found my voice. "It can't be true. I just spoke with her yesterday." I stopped, realizing how little sense that made, then forced myself to rally. "What do we know so far?"

"Very little. Marie was stabbed. She bled to death."

"Where?"

"In Montmartre," he told me, "not far from her home on the rue St. Roustique, behind the Place du Tertre."

"Is this where the body was found? On the rue St. Roustique?" I asked.

"Yes, but on the other side of the street. There is a small alley by the Auberge de la Bonne Franquette, at number 9. An employee of the Auberge found her when taking out the trash. He called for help, but it was too late. Marie died before they arrived."

"Perhaps she was in the alley in an attempt to lose somebody who was following her." I suggested.

"After what Marie told you yesterday, this may indeed be so."

"She also said she was in fear for her life."

"Sadly, she was correct."

"Perhaps the creep with the red tattoo was following her."

"That may be so. Let us hope we learn more when we arrive in Montmartre." A dark cloud passed over Béchard's face as the squad car sped off toward Montmartre.

# Chapter 21

The ride to Montmartre was a blur. Béchard shouted angry words into his phone, his voice competing with the blaring siren. My mind was mush, my body numb. This couldn't be happening. Marie couldn't be dead.

I had a serious talk with myself, trying to process the horror and sadness of three deaths in just a few days without allowing my past experiences to color my feelings now, or to determine my actions. I functioned one breath at a time—*thank you, yoga instructor*—working to control my emotions, or at least to turn them into something positive. Swallowing my sorrow, I resolved to be the tough professional I knew I could be and switched into full investigator mode. Besides, I didn't want Béchard to see me cry.

The police car deposited us in a small, narrow alleyway paved with cobblestones. Traffic was such that the driver suggested we'd do better on foot. My two-inch heels presented a challenge on the uneven pavement, but I struggled along and managed not to fall.

Béchard ushered me through the alley and onto the rue St. Roustique, where Marie had lived, a charming oasis lined with white stucco houses covered in ivy. Exactly what I had imagined to find in Montmartre. Except for the clamor of the police investigation in progress.

It was easy to spot the alley where Marie's body had been found, a small area behind the Auberge de la Bonne Franquette. Yellow tape hung across the entrance. A wooden gate squeaked open on its hinges; the stench of rotting garbage and something even worse—death, perhaps—permeated the air. Police technicians swarmed the area.

"Remain here," Béchard said as he stepped under the tape. I was fine with that. From where I stood, I could see all I wanted to see, and then some. I steeled my body, stilled my thoughts and surveyed the area.

The chalk marks on the ground where Marie's body had been gave me the willies. A large rust-colored spot stained the paving stones. I shuddered, realizing it was Marie's blood. My mind could see her lying there, dying. I fought back tears and concentrated on more constructive things. What had Marie been doing here? Was she trying to elude somebody following her? Did she come for a meeting? Or maybe to hide something, like the note?

Béchard exchanged words with another officer, made some notes, then returned to me. "I have seen enough here. The local police are scouring the area for anything which might be important. The investigation is under control. Let us pay a visit to Marie's concierge." He pointed across the street.

The building at #6 was lovely, three stories of white stucco, windows with iron grill-work and red geraniums spilling out of window boxes. The door was a beautiful dark wood with elaborate carvings, almost a medieval look. It suited the Marie that I knew.

Béchard approached the door and pressed the button.

A small woman with a mass of frizzy gray hair peered at us through the half-opened door. "What do you want?"

"Police." Béchard displayed his identification.

"*Encore*! / Again! Police, police and more police. All morning long. I have had enough police. Please leave me in peace to mourn my friend."

"*S'il vous plaît*, *Madame*, it is important that we speak with you," Béchard said.

"*Ah, oui*. Always important. But to whom?"

"I regret disturbing you, *Madame*, but there are a few questions…"

"Questions, always questions. Why can't you people leave us alone? I already told the others everything I know. Which is nothing."

I jumped in. "Please. I was a friend of Marie's." My voice quivered as I spoke.

The woman eyed me up and down. "How did you know her?"

"I worked with her at the dig, as a volunteer."

The scowl left her face. "So you're the one."

"I beg your pardon?"

"The new girl. The American with the Canadian accent. She liked you, you know. Said you had spunk. Felt she could trust you."

"Does that mean we may speak with you?" Béchard asked.

"I suppose it does." She stepped into the street. In full daylight, she looked even smaller and grayer—rather gnome-like. Her black dress, accompanied by black stockings and heavy black shoes, had been out of style for at least twenty years. Despite the August heat, she wore a sweater, also black, buttoned all the way to her neck. Her age was up for grabs.

Béchard pulled out his pen and notebook and began a barrage of questions. "Your full name, *Madame*?"

"Hélène Desmarais."

"You are the concierge of this building?"

"*Oui*."

"For how long?"

"Nearly thirty years."

"And Marie Duprès, how long did she live here?"

"Difficult to say. She was here when I arrived. Already established in the neighborhood."

"Did you know her well?"

"Everybody knew Marie. She was friendly, fun. One could not help but become her friend." The concierge's eyes filled up with tears.

"Did you know her family? Any relatives?" he asked.

"There was nobody. All dead in the war."

"Did Marie have many visitors?'

"*Ah, oui*, often."

"Were you familiar with these people?"

"*Bien sûr* / of course. They were neighbors, old friends. After so many years, one knows nearly everybody."

Béchard hesitated for a moment, then said, "So all her visitors tended to be…"

"Of a certain age? *Oui*. Marie was not a young woman. *Naturellement*, neither were her friends." She paused and knit her eyebrows. "There was that one young man the other day. I had not seen him before."

Béchard poised his pen. "A young man to see Marie? Someone from the dig, perhaps?"

Madame Desmarais gave this some thought. "*Non*. I do not believe so. His hands were soft, his fingernails clean. Not the hands of a digger."

"And this young man, what did he want?"

"To see Marie. That is all I know. I told him she was not here. He left."

"Can you tell us how he was dressed?" I broke in.

She responded slowly, "An ordinary shirt and trousers. Why do you ask?"

"Did the shirt have long or short sleeves?"

"They were long. I remember wondering why one that young would dress so on such a warm day." She glanced down at her own attire and blushed.

"Age?" Béchard asked.

"Everybody looks young to me."

Béchard frowned. "Perhaps around the same age as *Mademoiselle* Lynch?" he glanced in my direction.

The concierge nodded. I wondered how old either she or Béchard thought I was.

"Did anybody else visit Marie in the past few days?" Béchard continued.

"Visit, *non*."

"Or come to her apartment on business?" Béchard persisted.

"O*ui*. A man came by the other day, from the *compagnie de téléphone*. He was here only a short time. Marie was not at home. I let him in."

Béchard jumped to attention. "What did he want?"

"There was trouble with the lines. He needed to check the phone in Marie's apartment." The concierge folded her arms and looked up at Béchard. "I escorted him in and remained with him while he did so."

"Of course. Tell me what he did."

"He examined the phone. Took it apart, examined the pieces, put it back together. Then he left."

Béchard frowned. "Have you noticed any unusual vehicles in the neighborhood lately?"

"If you mean cars which don't belong here, *oui*. A black minivan. It is parked no matter where, blocking entrances up and down the street. The neighbors have been quite upset. We reported this to the local police, even gave them the registration number, but so far nothing has been done. Perhaps you could help us with that."

"I will look into this for you." Béchard made a note. "Did anybody see the owner of this van? Or converse with him?"

"People have knocked on the door, to ask that it be moved. Never a response."

I interrupted. "Did you see Marie much in the past few days? And speak with her?"

Madame Desmarais stared at me. "*Hélas, non.* And that is strange."

"Why so?" Béchard asked.

"For many years now, Marie would stop to visit with me upon returning home in the evening. She would speak about her day; I would speak of mine. We would have a coffee, or a glass of wine."

"And she didn't do that recently?" I asked.

"We spoke Tuesday evening. That is when she told me about you. But not since then."

Béchard spoke up. "Any idea why not?"

"She did not return at her usual hour. Marie was a woman with regular habits. Every night for many years, she returned home between 7:00 and 7:15 in the evening."

"This changed recently?" Béchard continued his questioning.

"*Oui*. On Wednesday, it was 2:00 a.m. when I heard her come in. The hinges on the front door are in need of oil. The squeak awakened me. I met Marie in the stairway to ask if she was all right."

"Was she?" I asked.

"So she said, but she did not look well. She told me she was tired, said we would talk the next evening. I looked forward to that. The wine was open, the glasses on the table. But she never came." The concierge bit her lip. "Marie was so close to home when she was attacked. It is frightening. This neighborhood has always been safe and peaceful."

"Madame, thank you for your time. You have been most helpful." Béchard closed his notebook and replaced it in his pocket.

"*De rien* / You're welcome. I hope it will assist you in finding the monster who did this. It is upsetting. A murder on one's own street." She turned the brass knob and ducked back in through the door.

Béchard and I headed up the street. "What do you deduce from what Madame Desmarais has told us?" he asked.

That was easy. "Marie was followed. Her phone was tapped. Perhaps by the same man who followed me? Perhaps not. We have no way to tell."

"True enough. I will arrange to have her phone checked for fingerprints, and for whatever device may have been attached to it." He checked his watch. "I wish to interview the restaurant employee who found Marie's body, but it is too early. The officer at the scene informed me this man would not arrive until noon."

I looked up the street, saw the shiny white dome of church of Sacré Coeur and had an idea. "As long as we have some time, would you like to visit the basilica? To say a prayer for Marie. And light a candle."

"And make three wishes?" He grinned.

"Let's both wish that we catch Marie's killer quickly."

# Chapter 22

Béchard and I entered the Auberge de la Bonne Franquette from the back door, Rue St. Roustique, to avoid the crowds of the Place du Tertre. It would have been pleasant to sit out front at one of the tables with blue and white striped umbrellas, but we needed a quiet place to interview the employee who had found Marie's body.

Our table was in a corner, in the rear, far away from the lunch crowd, which was already substantial even though it was barely noon. It was rather dark, a little stuffy, but definitely quiet.

The restaurant was old and fit well with my preconceived notion of what Montmartre should be. Worn wooden tables with candles for centerpieces gave it a rustic look in spite of the white linen tablecloths and napkins. The only thing missing was the sawdust on the floor.

"I don't want anything to eat," I announced. My repressed emotions had landed in my stomach, which was now doing flip flops and protesting the very thought of food.

"You must eat, *mon amie,*" Béchard said. "To maintain your strength, so we may continue our investigation. I am certain Marie would not want you to become ill with grief. I shall order something for you, perhaps a *croque-monsieur*. I guarantee you will find it tasty. And I shall have the same."

Arguing with him was useless. I acquiesced. And whatever a croquet-monsieur was, it had an intriguing name. The best translation I could come up with was Mr. Crunchy. *Hmmmm.*

The waiter approached with Béchard's wine and my beer. Béchard gave him the order then turned to me. "You have been most quiet since our visit to Sacré Coeur."

I sipped my beer, searching for a response which wouldn't expose the raw emotions I was struggling to keep in check. "I've just been thinking. Trying to figure out the missing link."

"The what?"

"The link—between the past and the present—which will make everything make sense." I stared into my beer.

We suspended our discussion while the waiter served our croques-monsieurs. They turned out to be the French version of a grilled ham and cheese sandwich. Their aroma was heaven-sent; it made me realize that I was hungry after all. Thank goodness I didn't pick mine up and dig in right away or it could have been embarrassing. Béchard attacked his with a knife and fork. The French seemed to have an aversion to eating with their fingers.

"Please, tell me more about this missing link." He drained his wine glass, then refilled it from a carafe on the table. I couldn't imagine how he could drink two glasses of wine at lunch time. That would put me to sleep for the entire afternoon.

"Consider the traitor," I said. "He has to be at least Marie's age, possibly older. Either late eighties or early nineties."

"Quite right."

"But the man who followed me was much younger than that. Absolutely no more than mid-thirties."

"So?"

"So how does he fit in here? He can't be the traitor. Is he working for him? Is he trying to protect the traitor?"

"*Helas*," he sighed, "I wish I knew. Perhaps when our computer search for criminals with red tattoos has been completed and we are able to locate this person ..."

"But what if you don't find him that way? Or what if you do find him, but there's no connection to the traitor? Or to the Résistance?"

"Then why was he following you? Is that what you mean?"

"Exactly. If this guy is totally unrelated to everything else that has happened, then I don't know what he wants with me. Either way, I don't like it."

Béchard swallowed another forkful of his sandwich.

I took a long, slow drink of my beer, then continued carving up my sandwich. I was tempted to use my fingers. The fork took so much longer, and I was hungrier than I had thought. But good manners prevailed.

The maître-d' approached our table, followed by a sheepish looking middle-aged man whom he introduced as Gaston Laurent, the employee who had found Marie's body. The maître-d' cast a disdainful look in Laurent's direction, and strolled off, nose in the air.

Laurent stood silently by our table, hands behind his back, shifting his weight from one foot to the other. The best word to describe him was scruffy. He was seriously in need of both a shave and a shampoo. His overalls were faded and torn, his apron stained. He stared at his feet, looking nothing like a waiter.

Béchard looked Laurent up and down, his eyes coming to rest on the overalls. "Please, seat yourself, *Monsieur* Laurent. I am most appreciative that you are willing to answer a few small questions for us. What are your duties here?"

Laurent sat opposite Béchard. He looked in my direction, though not exactly at me. "I wash the dishes after lunch and dinner, sweep up at night after closing, remove the trash. I am happy to do whatever needs doing. I cannot be particular, *vous savez*. I have six children to support. One must earn one's living as one can."

Béchard made a quick note. "It was while taking out the trash last night that you discovered the deceased?"

Laurent's eyes filled up, his lips quivered. He stared at his hands and said nothing for several moments. Finally, he raised his head. "I regret to confess that I had too much to drink and neglected to sweep up and remove the trash. It was, therefore, urgent for me to arrive early this morning and attend to these things. So I would not lose my job, *vous savez*."

"You have a key to the restaurant?"

"I did. This was necessary because I often close up after cleaning at night. But no more, *hélas*. The boss has now taken my key and threatened to dismiss me if I am discovered once more drinking on the job. He was kind to give me this one final chance."

"I see. Exactly what time was it when you arrived in the morning?"

Laurent fidgeted in his chair. "Between 6:15 and 6:30. The bells of Sacré Coeur had not yet rung the half hour."

"Tell me what happened. What you saw and heard. Anything unusual that you noticed. In short, anything which may have a bearing on this case."

"There is very little to relate, *Monsieur l'Inspecteur*. I unlocked the front door to the restaurant, completed the sweeping and cleaning. Then I removed the trash."

"You entered the back courtyard. Then what?"

"Then I saw her."

"Continue."

Laurent closed his eyes for a moment, then said, "She was lying on her side, facing away from me. At first, I didn't realize she was hurt. Thought she was a bum sleeping off a drunk. As I approached, I heard her moan."

"She was conscious when you first discovered her?" Béchard's eyes grew wide.

"Barely. I moved closer. To ask her to leave. To tell her this was private property and she was not allowed to sleep there. That is when I saw a pool of blood on the ground and realized that she was injured."

Béchard looked Laurent squarely in the face. "Go on."

"I ran inside the restaurant to call the ambulance, then returned to the courtyard and remained there with the lady until the ambulance arrived." Laurent leaned back in his chair.

"Was she still conscious at that time?" I asked him.

"*Oui, Madame*."

"Did she speak at all?"

He closed his eyes for a moment, then replied, "She moaned a lot, as if she were in a great deal of pain. And she kept mumbling something over and over. I regret to say I was unable to determine exactly what it was."

"Think about it, please," Béchard said. "Think hard."

And think he did, closing his eyes and scratching his head. After a full minute, he said, "*Eh bien*, as I told you, she was moaning and mumbling. The only thing I remember hearing her say was '*peche*'."

"*Peche*?" Béchard repeated as he wrote in his notebook.

"*Oui*. She said '*peche*'." He looked at us, then around the restaurant, then back at us.

"Did you see anybody else? On the rue St. Roustique or in the alley?"

"*Non, Monsieur*."

"Did you hear any unusual noises—footsteps, perhaps?"

"*Non, Monsieur*."

"Did you notice a purse nearby, or anything else the woman may have been carrying?"

Laurent shook his head.

Béchard closed his notebook. "Thank you for this information. I ask that you remain available should there be any additional questions."

"We are finished? I may leave?" Laurent leaped up from his chair and disappeared into the restaurant's kitchen.

Béchard signaled the waiter for the check, pulled some bills from his wallet and rose to leave without waiting for change. I followed him, mulling over the word "*peche*" and wondering why Marie had said it.

We headed up the alley to rejoin the squad car. I stumbled on the cobblestones and snapped off the heel of my right shoe. "Damn! These are my favorite dress shoes. And they're practically new!"

"At least we don't have far to walk."

I nodded and hobbled along behind him.

When we were in the car, I asked, "What do you think about Marie saying 'peche'?"

"Perhaps you should tell me what you think."

"Peche is an interesting word. Depending on which accent mark is used, it can mean fish, or peach or sin. What do you suppose Marie was trying to say?"

"We will probably never know," he replied. "Also, please consider that "peche" may have been only part of a word—perhaps "dépêchez" as in hurry. There are many possibilities." He retrieved his phone from his pocket. "Let us return to the Préfecture to attempt to identify your stalker."

"Would you mind if we stopped at the *pension* for a moment on the way? I need to change these shoes before I cause myself serious injury."

"*Pas de probleme* / Not a problem." He had a brief conversation with the driver, then the car sped off to the *pension*, this time without the siren.

# Chapter 23

"I'll just be a minute," I told Béchard when we reached the *pension*.

He nodded as I limped away on my broken shoe.

My Irish sense of fatalism caught up with me as I mounted the stairs to my room. The past few days had been beyond belief. Two people that I'd met, and liked, had been murdered. A tattooed man was following me. I'd ask myself what else could happen, but then it might. *Welcome to Paris, Amy Lynch. Have a wonderful time.*

If only Sam were here. He'd listen to my worries. He'd lick me, wag his tail, let me pet him. Just snuggle up and make me feel better. If Pete were here, he'd jump into action and be my hero, protecting me from harm, doing whatever he could to make me feel safe and happy. I missed the two males in my life. Wondering if Béchard could take their place, even just for now, I bumped right into the housekeeper in the hallway.

"*Pardon*, Elizabeth. I'm sorry. I wasn't paying attention."

"*Pas de problème, Mademoiselle.* / Not a problem." She began to walk away, then turned and said, "You missed your brother, *Mademoiselle* Amy. He could not wait any longer."

Her words stopped me dead in my tracks. "What did you say?"

"Your brother was here to see you. He waited as long as he could."

My heart pounded. I had no brother. Who the hell was here? And what did he want? "You're sure he said he was my brother?"

"*Oui, Mademoiselle*." She backed away a few steps, eyes wide.

"He asked for me by name?"

"*Mais oui, bien sûr*. After all, he is your brother." She headed down the hallway toward the kitchen.

My hands shaking, I fished the key from my shoulder bag and opened the door. Then my jaw dropped. And my blood pressure shot sky high.

"Béchard!" I shrieked as I ran down the stairs and out the door. "Béchard! Come here! Quickly."

He jumped from the squad car and joined me by the door. "What is it? What has happened? Are you all right?"

"A man was here looking for me. He told the housekeeper he was my brother. And he trashed my room." I struggled to regain my composure. It didn't work. Tears filled my eyes; my breath came in short, noisy gasps.

Béchard ran up the stairs. "Show me."

My voice failed me as I led him up the stairs and down the hallway and pointed into my room. The place was a shambles. The armoire was open, and empty, my clothes flung everywhere, cosmetics, books, papers were strewn all over the floor. The bed was torn apart, the mattress leaning against the chair. "See? See what he did! This is awful."

"The situation is most serious. Please wait here. Do not enter the room." He dashed down the stairs.

Alone in my doorway, I clenched my fists and forced myself to breathe. This couldn't be happening. Where the hell had Béchard gone? How could he leave me here just when I needed him the most?

I fought the urge to succumb to a total melt-down. Now was not the time. If I was in danger, it was crucial to pull myself together, to think, and act, rationally, not fall apart like a helpless wimp. And I had some serious questions for the housekeeper. "Elizabeth!" I shouted.

She appeared in the hallway.

"Did you let that man into my room?"

"*Ah, oui*, because he is your brother." She gave me a timid smile.

"But he's not. I don't have a brother. And look what he did to my room. Just look!" I struggled to rein in my anger. Or was it fear? Anger was the better choice. It would keep me strong.

Elizabeth peered into the room clutching a dishtowel in her hands, then shrank back. "Jésu! What happened?"

"That's what I'd like to know."

Béchard bounded up the stairs, followed by our driver. "Please step away, Amy. Officer Marchand must secure the area."

"He what?"

"He will guard the room, ensuring nothing is disturbed until the crime scene technicians arrive."

"Crime scene technicians?"

"*Mais oui*, to examine the room. To search for fingerprints and other evidence so we may identify the person who has done this."

I squirmed. My personal things—bras, panties—were everywhere. It was bad enough that awful man had gone through them. And now the police would do so as well. I knew it was standard operating procedure. I hated it anyway.

"Do not concern yourself about items which are of a personal nature," Béchard said, reading my mind yet again. "These men are professionals. They have no wish to invade your privacy; they simply need to do their job."

He took me by the elbow. "Please come with me."

He guided me down the hall and into the dining room. Seating himself, he indicated for me to do the same. “This is frightening for you, and dangerous. But, please, you must calm yourself so we may determine what has happened.”

Taking a long, ragged breath, I announced. “I’m calm.” I forced it to be so. “Where do we start?”

# Chapter 24

Béchard pulled his notebook from his pocket. "How, *s'il vous plaît*, was this person able to gain access to your room? Do you not lock the door when you leave?"

"He lied to Elizabeth. Said he was my brother. So she let him wait for me in the room."

Béchard beckoned to Elizabeth cowering in the doorway. She inched toward him and said "I was trying to be helpful."

"I see." He frowned. "So this man was American?"

"I think so," she stammered, not looking at Béchard.

"You think so? Did he speak with an American accent?"

"I guess so. *Hélas*, I do not know. My French is not so good, *Monsieur l'Inspecteur*, that my ear can distinguish accents. He was polite. He wished to surprise *Mademoiselle* Amy with his visit. That is all I know." She began to cry. "I intended to help. If *Madame* Hulot is told what I have done, she will dismiss me. And my husband Henrique as well."

"Nobody is accusing you of anything." Béchard's tone softened. "But we do require your assistance. Any information you can give us will help. I will be happy to report to *Madame* Hulot that you have been cooperative in providing the police with important information."

She dried her eyes and blew her nose into a dish towel.

The crime scene team arrived in the hallway, ushered in by Elizabeth's husband Henrique—three policemen armed with cameras, sketch pads, crime scene tape and other assorted paraphernalia. Béchard had a word with them in the hall, showed them to my crime scene, then returned to the dining room to question Elizabeth.

"So," Béchard began, "at what time did this man arrive?"

"A little before 10:00. *Mademoiselle* Amy had just left."

"Who answered the door?"

"I did. Henrique was at the other end of the hall, fixing a leaky faucet."

"So Henrique did not see this man?"

"*Non, Monsieur.*"

"What did the man say?"

"As I told you, he wished to see *Mademoiselle* Amy."

"He asked for her by name?"

Elizabeth nodded.

Béchard frowned. "What else did he say?"

"He wished to wait and surprise his sister."

"Whose idea was it for him to wait in her room?"

Elizabeth sucked in her breath. "His. I was cleaning the dining room to prepare for lunch. He said he did not wish to be in my way."

"So you unlocked the room and let him in." His tone was stern and clipped.

"*Hélas, oui.*" She hung her head.

"How long was he in there?"

"An hour or so, perhaps a bit more. He came to speak with me in the kitchen. Said he was unable to wait any longer and would I inform *Mademoiselle* Amy he would return later and hoped he would find her there at that time."

Béchard's head shot up. He glanced in my direction, but showed no other reaction.

*Son of a bitch*! The last thing I needed was for whoever it was to return and find me here. It was not yet mid-afternoon and already this was one of the worst days of my life.

"Elizabeth, can you describe this man?" Béchard asked.

"He was not old. Perhaps the same age as *Mademoiselle*."

"Early thirties?" he asked, smiling at me.

"*Oui, oui.*"

"Was he tall or short? Light or dark? Did he have a beard? A mustache? Did he wear glasses? What color was his hair?"

Elizabeth listened with a pained expression on her face. "His height was medium, his hair brown. Sadly, that is all I can remember."

I wracked my brain for something that would jar her memory. "How was he dressed?"

"Dressed? He wore dark trousers and a white shirt."

"His shirt, did it have long or short sleeves?"

"The sleeves were short." Elizabeth beamed. "Of this I am certain."

"And why," Béchard asked, "are you so certain?"

"Because I saw his tattoo. On his arm. Right here." She pointed to her left forearm.

Had to be my stalker. "Can you describe this tattoo?" I asked.

"Perhaps a rose. I am not sure. However, I am positive about the color. It was red."

Béchard put down his notebook. "Elizabeth, you have been very helpful. This is all the information we require of you at this time. I trust you will be available later, if the need arises?"

"Is it finished? Am I free to go?"

"*Mais oui.*"

Elizabeth rushed toward the doorway.

Her husband Henrique appeared on the scene "*Excusez-moi,* I do not wish to intrude, but is there a problem? May I be of some assistance?"

Béchard turned to Henrique. "Perhaps it would be good for your wife to get some fresh air. Why don't you take her for a nice long walk?" They were gone in an instant, speaking loudly in Portuguese.

"You are an excellent investigator," Béchard said to me.

"Why do you say that?"

"The shirt. This was the one question which elicited useful information. Very clever."

"Thanks. It's routine when questioning women. They notice clothing more than men do. I knew that if she thought about the shirt, she'd also remember the arm. And the tattoo."

"I commend your insight. Now we are not entirely in the dark. We are dealing with the same man who followed you yesterday. It is a start. I find it most disconcerting that he asked for you by name. And stated he will return."

"It's frightening. How could he know my name? And what does he want from me?"

Our conversation was interrupted by one of the crime scene technicians. "*Excusez-moi, Monsieur l'Inspecteur.* I need to speak with you concerning something we have found." He handed Béchard some papers in a large plastic bag. "We found these strewn on the floor. As they appeared to go together, we reassembled them, an easy task, since the pages are numbered."

"And?" A note of impatience crept into Béchard's voice.

"And page 9 is missing. We have searched the entire room. It is nowhere."

"May I see that?" I asked.

He handed me the pile of papers. It was the first fax I had sent to Nancy in the office. I scanned the documents to determine what was on the missing page 9. "Holy shit!"

"What is wrong?" Béchard asked.

"Page 9 was my copy of the note."

Béchard cursed under his breath. "This is what I feared. That note was the object of your stalker's search. That means he is indeed connected to the incident at the dig, and to the deaths of Toussaint, Moreau and Marie. We must conclude that somebody, somewhere, places a good deal of importance on this note. I must check at the office to learn if they have succeeded in decoding it yet. We must return to the Préfecture at once. While I am checking on things, you must review mug shots in the hope of identifying this man."

"Perhaps I should stay here this afternoon to put things back together once your officers are finished." And hopefully calm myself down. "Could somebody bring the mug shots here? Then Elizabeth and I could look at them together."

"*Non*. This person said he will return. It is unsafe for you to remain here."

"I can't let him scare me away. If I run and hide, he has won, whoever he is. I won't let that happen. It isn't fair."

"Fair is not the issue. This man has already killed three people. You are in danger. Your safety is the primary concern. And we must allow the technicians to conduct their investigation."

"But I have to call the office and update them."

"That can be done from the Préfecture."

I stood my ground. "I don't like being forced out of here. It's a sign of weakness."

"Or common sense. If this man returns, it could prove fatal."

"Why would he return? He already has what he came for."

"Perhaps simply to tie up loose ends. And eliminate them."

I agreed grudgingly. It was fine to object in principle, but my safety was another matter. I grabbed my shoulder bag. "All right. But only if one of the crime-scene technicians can get me a functional pair of shoes. I can't go out in these."

# Chapter 25

# Judas

Judas hung up the phone with a crash, almost breaking the hand piece. He clenched his fists and worked at breathing normally.

Philippe had done it again. Blown it. Oh, Marie was silenced, to be sure. But they were no closer to finding the note, original or copies. How could his son be so incompetent?

Philippe had pleaded his cause like the weakling he was. "Don't be angry, Papa. I did the best I could. It should have worked." He whimpered. "She was supposed to have it with her when she went out. She said so herself."

What had gone wrong? Was his son that stupid? Or was Marie more clever than he thought? Even in death, the woman had outwitted him. No matter about her now. She was gone, silenced forever.

Still, he wasn't safe. Philippe's source at the police said the American girl from the dig had a copy of the note as well. How many copies were there? The American had given one to the police. That had been easy enough for Philippe's source to locate and destroy. Now the nosy bitch had to be dealt with. Fast.

# Chapter 26

My fists unclenched and my anger began to dissipate around the time we passed the two armed guards at the *Préfecture de Police*. I knew I was safe—at least for a while. Now I was more angry than afraid.

Béchard ushered me to his desk and motioned for me to sit. He removed a mound of paperwork and placed it on top of a file cabinet. "Make yourself comfortable. I must leave you for a while, to check on several matters. Also to see if the sketch artist is available. When I return, I will bring *les photos d'identité judiciaire* / mug shots for you to examine."

Sitting there alone, I frowned. It is tough to be a cool, calm professional when you're involved personally. What I needed at the moment was my best friend. I calculated the time difference. 3:30 in Paris. Six hours. 9:30 A.M in Boston. Nancy should be at the office by now. I grabbed my cell and placed the call.

"Good morning. This is Nancy. May I help you?"

"I certainly hope so." My voice quavered in spite of myself.

"Amy? Is that you? You sound upset."

"Upset and then some. Marie Duprès has been murdered. My room has been ransacked by a tattooed man who has been stalking me."

"Oh my God! That's awful! Are you all right?"

"For the moment, yes. I'm at the police station. I need to pull myself together and focus."

"Focus on what?"

"On everything that has happened. It's all connected somehow. I need to figure it out."

"You're a lot braver than I am, Amy. Please be careful."

"What choice do I have?" I blew out a long, slow breath. "I take it you got my faxes."

"Fax*es*? What do you mean fax*es*?"

"What do you mean what do I mean? I mean: Did you get the faxes I sent you?" I was in no mood to mince words.

"You sent more than one?"

"Yes. One Wednesday, another on Thursday."

"I got Thursday's. With the police and coroner's reports. Impressive. Not only did you manage to get your hands on those reports in a foreign country, but I could actually read your handwriting. I didn't get a fax on Wednesday though. Are you sure it went through?"

"I have the confirmation. I can't imagine why you don't have it. I sent it specifically to your attention so it would be delivered to you hot off the fax machine."

Nancy sighed. "If this department had its own fax machine, as common sense says it should, I'd have your fax. My guess is that the geniuses in the mail room messed up again. I'll ask around and see if I can track it down."

"Good luck with that." I'd had experience with misrouted mail in the past. Not good.

"Thanks. What was in this fax?"

"My first report. Information I got from Marie Duprès and an archaeologist named Claude. You need to find it. Fast.

Because the man who ransacked my room took page 9 of that fax. A copy of an old hand-written note from World War II. It's in some kind of code. After this note was found, bad things began happening at the dig—Toussaint's death, Marie's death. People who have seen this note are dying."

"Good lord. That's frightening. It has to be on somebody's desk somewhere."

"At least the police have another copy. They're working now on decoding it." And I hoped they'd finish quickly.

"When they do, will it explain why people are dying at the dig?"

"I hope so. But I wanted to update you in the meantime and think about the business end of this mess. With Marie dead, I don't know who will be filing a claim. Or when. Or even if. And I'm too much in the thick of things to drop this investigation any time soon. Can you stonewall for a few days, just hang onto the information until a formal claim can be filed?"

"Sure thing. And I'll check on how the workers comp policy handles death due to murder. That's never come up before, and it certainly wasn't covered in our insurance classes."

That was all the business I could deal with for the moment. I needed to talk about something ordinary, something normal, something having nothing to do with the recent events in Paris. "What's happening with you and Mark?"

"Not a whole lot. Things are fine." She paused. "Oh, wait, there was one thing."

"What's that?"

"You remember that odd birthday gift my father-in-law gave me?"

"You mean that god-awful ugly old bracelet?"

"That's the one. He said it was his mother's. Anyway, I had it appraised to insure it. Turns out the bracelet is worth a small fortune."

"Wow! Good for you. Even if it is ugly." I looked up to see Béchard standing in the doorway. "I better go now. I'll check back with you in a day or so. Take care."

"And you be careful. I'm worried about you."

"I'm worried about me, too."

I rang off. How long had he been there?

# Chapter 27

Béchard deposited several tomes on the desk. "*Les photos d'identité judiciaire*," he announced. "Mug shots. Let us hope your stalker is among them."

I flipped through the first volume. "We can discuss the case while I look," I told him. "Did you learn anything more about Marie's death?"

"The report is simple. Marie was stabbed just below the heart. As we know, she was alive when discovered but died before the ambulance arrived. She had no purse with her. One may assume it was taken by her assailant." He frowned. "The body is about to be released by the morgue. It has been claimed by the woman from the dig named Solange Picard."

"Solange? I wonder why."

"I cannot tell you that. I can, however, inform you that *Mademoiselle* Picard is assuming responsibility for the burial. There will be a small service tomorrow at 10:00 at the cemetery in Montmartre. I trust you will accompany me there?"

"Tomorrow? Doesn't that seem rather fast?"

He shrugged in that stereotypic Gallic fashion.

A small service at the cemetery? That's all she gets? I sighed, thinking about the Irish wakes and funerals that were common for my family. Finishing with the second volume of mugshots, I announced. “No luck so far. Perhaps this goon doesn’t have a criminal record.”

“Let us hope he does. Continue looking, *s’il vous plaît*.” He pushed a third volume in my direction then produced a bottle of mineral water and poured us each a glassful.

I took a long slow drink. “So what do you think?”

“In light of the small amount of information available to us, it is difficult to formulate any useful theories at this time.”

“Spoken like a true policeman.” I smiled for the first time in hours. “How about looking at this from a different angle?”

“And what angle might that be?”

“Let’s do it ass-end-to.”

He raised an eyebrow. “I beg your pardon?”

“It’s an expression. Meaning to start at the other end of the problem.”

He leaned back in his chair, crossed his legs and gave me his full attention.

“We know what precipitated the recent events,” I began. “Marie’s involvement in the Résistance, the traitor, and the discovery of the coded note.”

“Agreed.”

“Somehow, the note got her killed.”

“Probably, but it is too soon to be certain.”

Ignoring his comment, I continued, “So if we can’t solve Marie’s murder from what happened last night, let’s do it from what happened years ago. You said yourself that the same person—most likely the traitor—could be responsible for the deaths of both Marie and Toussaint.”

“Do not forget Moreau.”

“Right. Let’s look into the past, into Marie’s involvement with the Résistance. Let’s check out the people with whom she worked back then.”

“Spoken like a true archaeologist. Looking to learn from the past.” He grinned. “Your suggestion is not without merit. But tell me, *s'il vous plaît*, how do you propose to identify and locate these former compatriots of Marie?"

"We'll read the book I bought yesterday. There's an entire chapter on the people in Marie's immediate group. Then we discover where they are now. Surely the police have resources available to locate people."

"We do. It may work, my friend."

"Let's hope so. When we're finished here, let's head back to the *pension* to get the book."

He shook his head. "I prefer to have the crime scene technicians bring it to us here so we may keep you safe."

I actually thumped my hand on the desk. "I can't stay here forever. If you're worried, why not assign somebody to watch the pension, at least for a day or so? That will keep me safe."

He was silent for several moments, then said. "Agreed. I shall arrange for that before we depart. I am pleased to see that you are still the competent claims investigator and not the frightened young woman you could have become after today's events. You are a strong person, *mon amie*."

"I do my best. What else did you do while I was speaking with my office?"

"I checked with our code experts on their progress."

"And…?"

He averted his eyes. "It pains me to tell you this, and alarms me more than I care to admit…"

"What? Tell me."

"Our copy of the note is missing."

*Damn!* "Missing as in misplaced?"

"One can hope. Or perhaps it has been stolen."

*Double damn!* "Somebody is stealing from the police?"

"Perhaps so. My hope is that it will resurface any time now. Otherwise, I would have grave concerns about internal security in my department. For now, let us dwell on other avenues of investigation."

"If you say so, but this doesn't feel good." I closed another volume of photos. "Sorry. No luck here either."

He frowned. "Our sketch artist is on his way here to work with you. Perhaps while you do so you could continue looking at more *photos d'identité* as well. I must leave you for a bit, to have a serious discussion with a subordinate and attempt to locate that damn note."

I spent about an hour working with the sketch artist. The final product bore a remarkable likeness to my stalker. There was a mug shot as well, which resembled him, a fellow named Albert Deland. He had a long and checkered history, but no mention of a tattoo. I reported this to Béchard upon his return.

"Perhaps *Monsieur* Deland obtained his tattoo after this photo was taken. We will investigate him. But first, we should telephone the *pension* to see if the technicians have completed their work. And to learn if your stalker has returned as he said he would."

"Excellent idea."

Béchard reached for the phone, had a rapid conversation with somebody, then hung up. "The crime scene team will be finished shortly. And I am pleased to report that your unwelcome visitor has not returned."

"That's a relief."

A cloud darkened his face. "Since we will have people watching the *pension*, it is probably now safe for you to return. However, I advise you to remain in your room after dinner and admit nobody who is not known to you." He folded his arms across his chest.

"Ordinarily, I'd say that sounded boring. Right now, a quiet evening alone in my room sounds like blessed relief. Is there somewhere I can buy a bottle of wine on the way back? It would help me to relax."

"I know just the place. It is *en route*. Shall we depart?"

I stuffed my notebook and pen into my shoulder bag and rose to follow him. Once outside, we walked slowly along the Seine, saying little. We made a quick stop in a little wine shop nestled between a book store and a small café. I purchased a bottle of Chenin Blanc recommended by Béchard, as well as a corkscrew.

As we neared the *pension*, I broke the silence. "I need to tell you something. Nancy never got my first fax, the one I sent on Wednesday. She received the fax I sent from your office Thursday, but the first one, with a copy of the note in it, seems to be missing."

"How is that possible?"

"With our mail room, anything is possible. The fax may turn up shortly on somebody else's desk. But it is unsettling."

He furrowed his brow, but didn't pursue the subject.

When we arrived at the *pension*, Béchard had a word with the technicians who were on their way out. He showed Elizabeth the sketch of my stalker. She confirmed that is was indeed him, then disappeared quickly.

"You are certain you will be all right?" Béchard asked at my door.

"I'll be fine. I don't believe that man will return. Like you said, he got what he came for. I'll finish straightening up, have some wine and go to bed early. Don't worry." I handed him the book on the *Résistance Parisienne*. "Let's hope this contains something helpful."

"I shall be here at 9:30 tomorrow morning to escort you to the funeral of Marie."

"Sounds fine. See you then." I closed my door.

*Hell of a thing. All my dates with the man were for funerals.*

# Chapter 28

I looked around my room and groaned. So much to do, so much to consider, so much to worry about. I quickly remade the bed then flopped onto it and stared at the ceiling. A shiver ran up my spine. The room felt eerie, as if my stalker's presence somehow tainted the air.

This really sucked. It wasn't fair that he should make me feel out of place in my own room, my home for the next few weeks, such as it was. That would mean he had won. I wasn't about to let that happen.

I sat straight up. *This is my room, damn it,* I told myself. *He's gone. He's not coming back. That's all there is to it.*

I grabbed the bottle of wine and struggled with the corkscrew. Pete always teased me about my ineptitude at opening wine, as Danny had before him. The corkscrew Béchard had selected was unfamiliar and tricky to maneuver. It was a few minutes before I met with success.

Sitting down on the bed, mugful of wine in hand, I took a tasty gulp. And another. Then I refilled the mug. It was good to relax. The next thing I knew, the ringing of my cell phone awakened me.

"Hello?"

"How are you? You sound as if you're just waking up."

It was Nancy.

"I'm all right. Just exhausted from the day's events, not to mention almost an entire bottle of excellent wine. But why are you calling? Didn't I speak with you a couple of hours ago?

"This is a semi-official business call. And you're not going to like it."

"What do you mean?" I yawned.

"For starters, I got your first fax not long after I hung up from you earlier. Believe it or not, it was delivered to my father-in-law. The mail room never looked at the first name, just saw the name Fisher and delivered it straight to Executive Heaven. Then, from what I hear, all hell broke loose. Old man Fisher stormed down to Underwriting and demanded the file on the dig. He went ballistic, said we never should have written the policy."

"What does he care as long as it makes him money?"

"Beats me. Personally, I think the man is just plain losing it. It's time for him to retire. Anyway, Fisher sent the fax down to me in the inter-office mail. Which means it ended up on Mitch's desk today. Then Mitch was tied up in a budget meeting all morning and was late with the mail."

"That's a relief. Please make a copy of it at once. Make several copies and put them someplace safe. Whatever you do, don't lose them. I'll need you to fax page 9 back to me tomorrow."

"I may not be able to do that."

"Why not?"

"Mitch's being a real pain in the ass at the moment. You're off the case. No claim has been filed, so he says there's nothing to investigate."

"You're kidding."

"No. He calls it cost containment. Insists that the expense to coordinate with a French investigator is prohibitive. So he told me—and I quote—to forget all this investigation nonsense because there is no fucking claim. Sadly, he is the boss."

"He said 'fuck'? In the office?"

"That's right. I nearly died. I tried to tell him you were already there investigating, that you had police connections and we expected a claim to be filed any time now. He wasn't in a mood to listen. Just took the file off my desk and strutted away."

It was an interesting scene to picture. Laughable, but not funny. It also meant that Nancy no longer had page 9, the copy of the note, to send to me. "That stinks, Nancy, but he is the boss. Maybe you better do what he wants. Just drop it." I didn't mean any of that, but it seemed like the thing to say.

"You've got to be joking. What'll happen when the claim finally gets filed? We'll have lost valuable time. I don't feel right about this. I'll try to get Mitch to listen long enough to tell him you're on the scene and on top of things."

"Good luck with that," I said. "We know what a stubborn ass he can be. I'll continue to investigate anyway. This whole mess has become too personal for me not to."

"Good for you. I'll take anything you can get. We'll keep things quiet, sit on the information until it's needed. How's that?"

"Works for me. Let's you and I go out in style. Do an all-out investigation. We'll document the file, have it ready when needed. That'll keep our professional integrity intact. Maybe help me in finding my next job."

"And mine, too," Nancy added.

"Is this going to make things awkward for you? You're right there. And married to the boss's son. It's a lot easier to be bold when you're three thousand miles away like me."

"Not to worry. I'll be fine. Better to cover my professional ass. At the worst, I'll be wasting my time."

"Agreed."

"Listen, I better go. The pile of work on my desk is getting taller by the minute. Let me know as soon as you have anything concrete."

"Will do." I hung up, eager to continue my investigation. And to save both of our jobs.

# Chapter 29

Another early morning. I had been in Paris a week now. It seemed more like a lifetime, and not a happy one.

I had always wanted to visit Montmartre, the center of French art in the early twentieth century, the birthplace of Impressionism. When we were here the other day, we hadn't even entered the square, just concentrated on speaking with Marie's concierge. Now, as Béchard steered me through the crowds, I drank in the vibrant scene—artists busy at work on the sidewalks, cafés and souvenir shops with colorful awnings, throngs of tourists everywhere, a totally honky-tonk atmosphere. I was finally here—to attend a funeral. I sighed and followed Béchard.

The cemetery was a peaceful retreat with maple and chestnut trees providing an abundance of shade. Elaborate funeral monuments and decorative little chapels crowded the rolling landscape as far as my eyes could see. Marie's gravesite was simpler than most, next to that of her husband Jean under an ancient chestnut tree.

I checked my watch. Five minutes until the ceremony began. We were not the first to arrive. I watched Béchard scan the mourners and survey the area.

"I would like to position ourselves over there." He pointed to a small rise to the left. "This will afford us the opportunity both to hear the service and to observe the mourners with an unobstructed view."

When we reached the spot, I searched the crowd for familiar faces. André, Solange, Claude, and a few others I recognized from the dig whose names I didn't know. I pointed them out to Béchard. Several middle-aged men in well-cut suits stood together off to one side. From the Ministry, I assumed. The rest of the mourners were well over 60 and not so well-dressed. I didn't see my tattooed stalker among them.

Marie's farewell was simple but touching. A man from the Ministry spoke of her many years of service. He praised her work. An older man in a shiny blue suit talked of her days in the *Résistance* and the many lives she saved. His voice quivered, nearly failed him once or twice. He never looked up as he spoke, just concentrated on the notes grasped in his crooked fingers. Solange wept throughout.

The service was over in less than an hour. The mourners began to disperse. I looked to Béchard for a signal that we, too, would depart. His gaze was trained on the older man who had spoken of the *Résistance*. Béchard signaled to him. The man turned his head away and continued out of the cemetery. Béchard quickened his pace and caught up with him by the gate. "I regret disturbing you on such a sad occasion, *Monsieur*, but I must have a word with you. I am Inspecteur Paul Béchard." He displayed his identification.

"*Ah, oui,*" was the response.

"May I ask your name, please?"

"Gérard Renoud."

I recognized the name from the book I had purchased.

"You knew Marie from the war? From her work in the Résistance?"

"Oui, M*onsieur l'Inspecteur*. We worked closely together. Until her arrest." He shifted from one foot to the other.

"Do you have time to discuss Marie with us? Perhaps someplace away from here?"

"I suppose I must." Renoud checked his watch. "You may come with me now to my apartment, if you wish. However, our meeting must be brief. I am leaving at noon for a 1:00 appointment." He headed out of the cemetery.

We followed him up the street, arriving at the top of a steep incline.

"Is this a stairway or a street?" I asked Béchard.

"Both. It is a pedestrian stairway. A safer, less strenuous way to descend the hill. Most convenient, *n'est-ce pas*?"

The three of us were silent as we descended to the rue Gabrielle. The neighborhood was nowhere near as charming as Marie's. Old, shabby buildings, no window boxes, no flowers, everything in need of paint. Renoud lived at number 27, a five-story white structure with a café on the ground floor.

Renoud's apartment, up three flights of stairs, contained a beat-up old couch of indeterminate color and pattern, an overstuffed chair occupied by a fat tabby cat, a wooden table and three mismatched chairs. A hot plate and half-size refrigerator sat in the corner. Despite the warm day, the shutters were closed, adding to the dismal pall of the room. The scents of stale alcohol and Gauloise cigarettes pervaded the air. A sad place to spend one's old age.

We sat at the table. Renoud produced a bottle of cognac and three chipped jelly glasses. Not my beverage of choice, particularly in the middle of the morning, but it would be rude to refuse his hospitality. He raised his glass in silent toast— most likely to Marie.

"I apologize for intruding on your grief so soon after Marie's funeral," Béchard began.

"It was a lovely ceremony," I added.

Renoud lowered his eyes. "*Oui Mademoiselle*, the ceremony was fitting, exactly as Marie would have wished."

"Your eulogy was very moving," I told him.

"*Merci*. I did my best."

Béchard reached for his ever-present notebook and pen. "You knew Marie well?"

"Ah, *oui*. For many years." Renoud's eyes filled up. "We were the best of friends. At my age, one comes to treasure such friends. Those who knew you in your youth will forgive you much in your later years." His hand shook slightly as he reached for his glass. He downed the contents in a single gulp.

I gave him what I hoped was a kind, encouraging smile. "Did you meet Marie while working in the Résistance?"

"*Non*, quite the opposite. It was through my acquaintance with Marie that I became involved. Her husband Jean and I were in the same unit in the army. We returned to Paris together, defeated and discouraged, at the beginning of the Occupation. It was through him I came to know Marie. When Jean was conscripted for forced labor in Germany, it was I who brought her the sad news. Her husband was taken so quickly he was not given the opportunity to say good-bye." Renoud refilled his glass.

Béchard spoke up. "How were you able to escape a similar fate?"

"Before the war, I was a minor bureaucrat in Paris. The Germans had a need for the services I could provide. I despised serving the bastards who had conquered us. Marie convinced me to do so. She showed me how I could be of great service to those who wished to resist. And so I was." He stared at his hands.

Béchard scribbled in his notebook.

Renoud took a swig of his cognac. "There was a time when I wished Marie and I could be more than friends. I was very much in love with her. *Hélas*, she always mourned for her Jean. No other could take his place."

The cat jumped into Renoud's lap and stared at us through unblinking eyes.

"Marie told me something of those days." I said. "She made them sound incredible—dangerous and exciting at the same time. The work you did was so important."

"You are most kind, *Mademoiselle*. One did what one could in those difficult times. Often that was little enough. We were all so young, and in the middle of a nightmare from which one felt one would never awaken."

"Were you involved with the forged passports Marie smuggled into Paris?"

"*Oui*." Renoud sighed, and stroked the cat. "The office where I worked handled the location and documentation of citizens of Jewish ancestry. I had access to much information. We made full use of it. My job for the Résistance was to identify those who would be given the passports, who would have a chance for freedom. I obtained photos, handled distribution. For months I led a double life, appearing to work with the Germans while in fact spying on them. I felt the shame imposed upon me by those who did not know the true nature of my work, who treated me as a traitor. Marie gave me the courage to continue. Together we saved many people. At least for a while." His voice grew stronger. He raised his head and looked us in the eyes.

"What happened to change this?" Béchard asked.

"Things began going wrong. Marie was detained while returning to Paris. The passports were found. She was arrested. I went into hiding, unable to return to work for fear of arrest. Not knowing if Marie had revealed our names under torture. I regret to tell you I was a coward. My fears overcame me. I remained in hiding. To this day, I live with the shame of my weakness, my lack of courage."

"Marie never did reveal your names," I said.

"*Non*," Renoud smiled. "Such a strong woman, brave and determined. She never betrayed us." He pushed the cat off his lap and refilled his glass.

"What became of the others in your group?" I asked.

"They continued to work, though in a different endeavor. It was not easy to locate another group with which to work. Trust was a rare commodity in those days. Eventually they joined up with Claude and Chantal's group. I cannot tell you more than that. Their work was most secret, *vous savez*."

"Are you still in contact with any of them?" I asked.

"Only Henri. And now that we are no longer young and he is not well, our visits have become infrequent."

"Was Henri at the funeral service today?" Béchard asked.

"*Ah, non*, his health would not permit the trip here." He stared into his glass.

I changed the subject. "Had you spoken with Marie recently?"

"*Ah, oui*. She telephoned me Monday evening, to inform me of the death of Moreau."

Béchard broke in. "You knew Moreau?"

"*Bien sûr* / of course. He worked with us. He was the expert with codes."

"What did Marie say about his death?" I asked.

"It frightened her. It awakened a ghost from the past, the ghost of the traitor."

"Marie spoke to me of this traitor," I said. "She told me he was never identified."

"We suspected a fellow named Antoine. We accused him, then shot him. But we were mistaken. Our problems continued. The thought of this traitor has haunted me ever since. My one wish before I die is to identify and punish the monster who betrayed us in so many ways. This time I will not be a coward." He folded his arms across his chest.

Béchard looked up from his notes. "How did the death of Moreau relate to this traitor?"

I held my tongue, curious to see if Renoud told the same story I had heard from Marie.

"Something had been uncovered at the dig," Renoud said. "A coded note from the time of the Occupation. Marie brought it to Moreau for help in deciphering it. Apparently he was successful. On the evening of Marie's death, she told me Moreau had discovered the identity of the traitor, may he rot in hell."

Renoud took a long deep breath. "She said Moreau had telephoned this person, threatened to expose his crimes. This cost Moreau his life."

"So who was the traitor?" I asked.

"I do not know. Marie would not discuss it on the phone. She was coming to tell me in person when she was killed." He swiped at a tear with the back of his hand.

"Did she give you any indication? Did you have any suspicions?" I asked.

"*Hélas, non.*"

Béchard spoke up. "Have you spoken with any of the others since Marie's death?"

"Only Henri. And I will visit him today, at 1:00, to tell him about the service, who was there, what was said. It is sad when one's age and health prevent you from saying good-bye to old friends." Renoud filled his glass yet again and lifted it in another silent toast.

Béchard and I joined him.

"One last thing," Béchard said. "I would very much like to speak with Henri. Would it be possible for you to arrange a meeting for us?"

"I shall do what I can. Henri sees few people these days, due to his failing health. May I contact you later, after our visit, and let you know?"

"*Bien sûr* / of course." Béchard gave Renoud his card, adding both of our cell numbers.

Renoud stumbled slightly as he escorted us to the door. He made no attempt to see us down the stairs.

"I could cry for Renoud," I said as we walked. "Such a pathetic old man. So very alone. Ashamed of his cowardice during the war, finding consolation in a bottle of cognac and a cat."

Béchard gave me a mournful smile. "The man has, however, provided us with information which may prove useful. It should be interesting to speak with Henri."

An odd thought popped into my head. I mumbled "Rosebud" under my breath.

Béchard gave me a curious look. "What was that? I did not hear what you said."

My cheeks grew hot. "Oh, nothing."

He stopped and looked at me. "You said something."

"Just 'Rosebud'."

"Rosebud? Why would you say such a thing?"

"I was thinking of the movie Citizen Kane. Have you seen it?"

"Many times. Rosebud was the dying word of Mr. Kane, *n'est-ce pas*?"

"That's right."

"And this one word forms the basis for the plot of the film."

"Yes."

"Are you thinking about the word 'peche', wondering if it will assume a similar role in our investigation?"

"You never know."

"Do not forget, there are other possibilities we must consider."

"Such as?"

"Perhaps Gaston Laurent made that up simply to be finished with us."

"You may be right. But it seems like a good clue."

"It may still prove to be so. I must return to my office now to attempt to access Moreau's telephone records. They may identify the traitor. I will telephone you later about our meeting with Henri. Will you return to your *pension* now?"

"No way. I won't be like Renoud, shut up in his sad little room because he's afraid. I'm not going to let fear control me. I'm going to stroll down the Champs-Elysées and pretend I'm a normal tourist visiting Paris, maybe do some shopping. Anything to distract my mind for a couple of hours."

We headed off in opposite directions.

# Chapter 30

Pete called that evening while he was walking with Sam. The court case was over. His side won. I congratulated him then updated him on events. We made plans for him to fly to Paris and spend the remainder of my vacation with me. After the chaos and drama of the last few weeks, that would be blessed relief.

I spent the next morning updating my file for the anticipated claim. Info on Toussaint's funeral, Marie's death and our visit with Renoud. I put my report in an envelope addressed to Nancy at her home, and still marked it "Personal and Confidential." No way I wanted anybody at the office to know I was still working on the case or that Nancy was helping me.

Next, I grabbed my phone and dialed Peggy, just to check in with her, hear a friendly voice, maybe say hello to Sam.

"Good morning," she greeted me, her voice husky with sleep. "You sure are up early."

"Or perhaps you're sleeping late."

"There is a time difference, you know," she said.

"I thought I'd factored that in."

"Think again. Actually, it's good for you to get me up. Sam must be eager for his breakfast and a walk."

I closed my eyes, missing my good buddy. "How is my buddy doing?"

"Great. Pete comes by every day to walk with him, which is a big help because I'm putting in lots of extra time at work. Things are crazy busy."

*Ouch!* I hoped that wasn't because I was away. "Is everybody still furious with me?"

"Not everybody. Ever since Old Man Fisher took his nutty over you, the people who report to you have rallied to your defense."

"That's nice to hear. Thanks."

"You're welcome. Now, tell me about this French policeman you're working with. What's he like?"

"Pleasant. Professional. Quite formal, actually." *And cute as can be.*

"Young or old?"

"Middle-aged."

"Should Pete worry about the two of you?"

"No way. Our relationship is strictly business. Pete has nothing to worry about." I didn't usually lie to Peggy, but now seemed like a good time. She didn't need to know about my attraction to Béchard, let alone the guilt that accompanied it. "Give my love to Sam." We chatted for a bit, then I ended the call before she could ask me any more questions. Time to get ready to visit Henri. Béchard was due shortly.

As expected, he arrived precisely on time. "You look quite lovely."

I was pleased he noticed. "Thanks. I bought this dress yesterday. I was getting tired of the blue one. Wanted something different to wear to Henri's."

"Shall we depart?"

"Did you speak with Henri?" I asked as we stepped out into the street.

"*Non.* Renoud called to inform me Henri is willing to speak with us. He expects us between 2:30 and 3:00. Renoud cautioned me we must not remain any longer than necessary. Henri isn't well. He tires easily."

"I hope he doesn't live far. It's nearly 2:15 now. Are we walking?"

"*Pas de probeme* / not a problem. He lives off the Place de la Sorbonne, on the rue Chapollon. An easy walk from here. Was your afternoon enjoyable yesterday?"

"Very. I strolled down the Champs-Elysées, did some shopping. Then my boyfriend Pete called. He was walking with Sam. It was good to hear his voice."

"Pete's or Sam's?"

"Both, although with Sam I did most of the talking. He's an excellent listener. I miss him. We've been roommates for four years." Since just before Danny's accident. His death. Sam was Danny's last gift to me.

"Four years is longer than some marriages. Are Pete and Sam good friends?"

"Of course. You know what they say."

"I'm afraid I don't."

"Love me, love my dog."

"They say this?" He laughed.

We arrived at the rue Champollon, a narrow old side street devoid of sunlight and in a state of disrepair. The three-story stucco buildings were stained, chipped and in need of a good sand blasting.

The door at number 15, in marked contrast, was newly-painted in a muted teal blue. The name plate and door knobs were highly-polished brass.

The concierge, a frumpy middle-aged woman with mousey brown hair and a sour look on her face, answered our knock. She escorted us up the two flights of stairs to Henri's apartment.

We made our introductions at the door. Henri was a tiny shell of a man—withered, gray, feeble. He leaned on a cane as he ushered us into his sitting room.

Unlike the sad sparseness of Renoud's apartment, Henri's home was replete with memorabilia, possibly all that remained of his life. The living room was hot and stuffy, the windows shut on a beautiful day.

Henri must have read my mind. "I hope the warmth of the room is not uncomfortable for you. My health is not good. Even the smallest breeze afflicts me with chills."

"No need to apologize," Béchard replied. "We are pleased you are willing to give us some time."

"Time is all I have left to give. And I have not much of that." He sat in an overstuffed chair and motioned us toward the love seat. "How may I be of help?"

Béchard pulled out his notebook. "We are investigating the death of Marie Duprès."

I added, "Can you tell us about her past? About your work with her in the Résistance?"

"Marie," he sighed. "Beautiful, charming Marie. So full of life. No matter how bad the situation became, Marie was always cheerful, always helpful. She held our group together, gave us the will to continue. So sad that she is gone."

"You were fond of her?" Béchard asked.

"Fond, *oui*. But not like Renoud. He was a lovesick puppy, always gazing at Marie with big mournful eyes. As if she would betray the memory of her Jean with the likes of Renoud."

"The three of you worked closely together?" I asked.

"More than three. There were others—Chrétien, Katya, Dominique, Jean-Paul. One must not forget Jean-Paul. He was the strongest of us, the bravest."

Béchard poised his pen. "What were their last names?"

Henri closed his eyes. "*Voyons* / Let me see. Katya Beaumont. Jean-Paul Pecheur. As for Chrétien and Dominique, I do not know."

My back stiffened upon hearing "Pecheur." I turned to Béchard.

He shook his head in my direction, then continued his questioning. "After Marie's arrest, your group disbanded, *n'est-ce pas* / correct?"

"*Oui*. It was the end of so much. We did well, *vous savez*, saving many people with the passports Marie obtained. It was often difficult, but we did what we could."

"You were heroes," Béchard told him.

Henri continued. "After Marie's arrest, we lost our heart. And poor Renoud lost his nerve. So sad."

"How so?" I asked.

"The man had the soul of a coward. Only Marie's spirit gave him courage. He hated being regarded as a collaborator by those who didn't know the true nature of his work. He could only cope with Marie to sustain him. With her gone, he could not bear the shame. Or the fear."

"He left your group?" Béchard asked.

"Our group, his job, he left everything. Disappeared. The Germans questioned his friends, his neighbors. Nobody knew where he was. Poor Renoud. So afraid, so ashamed. The memories still haunt him."

"And the rest of you? What did you do then?"

Rather than respond to this, Henri said, "I am forgetting my manners. Such a poor host. May I offer you some wine?"

Béchard frowned.

I forced a smile. "That would be nice. May I help you?"

"I would be grateful for your assistance. I have few guests these days. Mostly just Renoud. And he helps himself. I keep the wine here for him. You know he drinks too much?" Henri struggled to his feet.

I followed him into the kitchen.

We returned with a bottle of Bordeaux and three crystal glasses, so different from Renoud's old jelly glasses.

Béchard helped me pour the wine, then continued his questions. "You were about to tell us what the rest of you did after Marie was arrested and Renoud went into hiding."

Henri's eyelids drooped, then closed. When he opened them, he had a faraway look in his eyes. "We joined another group. This was not easy. So much suspicion and mistrust. One was constantly in danger of being betrayed. But it was important to us to continue our work, though in a different way."

"Different how?" Béchard asked.

"No more passports. We smuggled people. Helped them sneak out right under the noses of the Germans. Got them to Vichy, in unoccupied France, through the château at Chenonceau."

That rang a bell in my head. What was it about Chenonceau? "Is that the château with the long gallery that spans the river?"

Béchard's face lit up. "*Ah, oui*, I remember. The location was unique. The building itself sat in occupied France. But the south door of the gallery, on the other side of the river, opened onto the free zone."

"Correct. Our plan worked at first. Well enough to convince us to send through more and more people. Then a few were caught, but not enough to scare us into discontinuing our operation. Then, toward the end, group after group, hundreds of people who should have escaped were all caught, all deported, all dead."

Henri's eyes darkened. "These people trusted us, depended upon us for their very lives. We worked hard to save them, only to see ourselves betrayed."

"What happened??" Béchard asked.

"The refugees arrived in Vichy, thinking they were free, that the nightmare was over, only to be arrested and transported to Germany, which is to say, killed."

"How awful," was all I could say in response.

"More awful than you will ever know. This could only have occurred if a traitor was providing the Germans with information. Someone from our group must have been working with René Bousquet. The worm, the cockroach, a man not fit to be part of the human race."

"I am familiar with the name," Béchard said. "I thought he had been cleared of the charges of crimes against humanity."

"A travesty of justice." Henri's voice rose. "Toward the end, when the Allies were on the verge of liberating Paris, Bousquet was instrumental in preventing the executions of several members of the Résistance. For this, they pardoned him the rest. Even though he was responsible for the deportation of 76,000 Jews, only 2,500 of whom survived."

"Who was involved in this second group?" I asked.

"*Voyons* / let's see. Dominique, Chantal, Jean-Paul, Chrétien, Katya, Bernard...."

Béchard took notes furiously. "Was Bernard at Marie's funeral this morning?"

"*Oui*. Renoud told me he was there. A strange fellow, kept to himself. He was part of my original group. Also of the second. I always suspected he was the traitor."

"Do you remember his last name?" Béchard asked.

Henri frowned at him. "Of course I do. I'm not senile yet. It is Laurencin."

"Does he live in Paris?"

"*Qui sait*? / Who knows? It has been years since anybody heard from him. I was surprised to hear he showed up at the funeral."

Béchard scanned his notes. "And Chantal and Katya? What can you tell us about them?"

"Chantal." Henri smiled. "Such a beauty. Soft golden hair. And spirit. There was fire in her very soul."

"What's her last name?" I asked.

"Parmentier. She's gone for many years. Cancer. A pity. She died so young, leaving her husband to raise a child alone. It was a tragedy."

"She left a child?" I asked.

"Didn't I just tell you that?"

"What became of him?" Béchard asked.

"Her. It was a girl. Christine. She was as beautiful as her mother."

"Was?" I asked.

"*Helas, oui*. She and her husband, Étienne, both gone. Killed in a traffic accident. So senseless. So sad. And with their baby only six months old."

Béchard turned to a new page in his notebook. "What became of this baby?"

"Marie raised her, of course. I thought everyone knew that. After all, it was Marie who was driving at the time of the accident. Took the girl in, raised the child as her own. And it wasn't out of guilt. Marie was a good, caring woman. She educated the girl, got her a job, loved her as any mother would do."

Something clicked in my mind. "Did she become an archaeologist like Marie?"

"Of course she did. Solange worshipped Marie. She wished to follow in her footsteps."

I turned to Béchard but he avoided my eyes.

He studied his notes for a moment before speaking. "And the other woman, Katya? Unusual name. Was she foreign?"

"Katya was a *sobriquet*, her nickname. I cannot recall her actual name."

"What became of her?" Béchard asked.

"Dead as well. Dead as can be. Dead as I'll be before long. Happens to us all, the good and the bad." He stopped speaking and seemed to wither before our eyes.

"Did Katya die in the war?" I asked.

"*Mais non.*" He jerked himself to attention. "Jean-Paul watched out for her. He protected her. They were lovers, *vous savez.*"

"Did they remain together after the war?" I asked.

"Of course not. How could they? Jean-Paul had to leave. His life was in danger. I saved him. Couldn't let a great hero like Jean-Paul fall into the hands of the Germans. He was my friend."

"How did you save him?" Béchard asked.

"I got him to Chenonceau when the route was still secure. I drove Jean-Paul there in the trunk of my car. Then my cousin got him through the château. And I kept my promise to him, for all these years, for as long as I could."

"What promise was that?" Béchard asked.

"To look after Katya. I promised to take care of her, to ensure she came to no harm, to protect her no matter what. He loved her so much. It pained him to leave her."

"Why didn't she escape with him?"

"She refused to leave. The journey was dangerous, and she was with child."

This caught Béchard's attention. "Jean-Paul's child?"

"B*ien sûr*. But he didn't know it when he left. She kept her pregnancy secret from him, to protect the man she loved."

"How beautiful," I said, "and how tragic."

Henri gave me an odd look. "Why? They all ended up all right, didn't they? Jean-Paul was safe. He made a lot of money. He supported Katya and the child. They never wanted for anything. What is so sad about that?"

"So he came back to France?" I asked.

"*Non, non*. He couldn't do that. Too dangerous for him if his work in the Résistance came to light. But he remained in contact with her, through a mutual friend. Used him as a conduit to send money for Katya and the child."

"Can you tell us who this conduit was?" Béchard asked.

"One of the code specialists. Someone I barely knew. I believe his name was Moreau."

Béchard chimed in. "So Jean-Paul kept in touch with Katya through Moreau?"

Henri sighed. "*Oui*. Also, sometimes Jean-Paul would telephone Katya, I got news of him from her. But I never told anyone, not even Renoud. I kept my promise to them. I kept their secret." His chin dropped to his chest; his shoulders sagged, as if suddenly bereft of energy.

"To summarize, Jean-Paul made a large amount of money, which he shared with Katya and their child, but he never returned to France." Béchard said.

"*Oui, oui*. I have already told you that. Have you not been listening?"

Béchard continued. "Do you know how he made his money? Or where he has been living all this time?"

"Only Moreau knew. He's the only one. Not even Katya. It was for Jean-Paul's safety. He changed his name, became a different person. But he never forgot his love for Katya. Took care of her until the day she died."

"When did she die?" I asked.

"Ten or twelve years ago. At my age, one begins to lose track. One year is much like the next. Anyway, she's gone now. And soon enough."

"Soon enough for what?" Béchard said, never raising his eyes from his notes.

"Soon enough so she never saw what became of that son of hers. We tried with him, both of us, for years and years, but he was no good. Once Katya was gone, I never saw the boy again. But I heard things. *Ah, oui*, I heard. He fell in with a bad crowd.

He was arrested more than once. For all I know, he may be in prison now. And good enough for him." Henri lowered his head.

"What is his name, this son?" Béchard asked.

"Philippe. Philippe Beaumont." Henri shook his head. "No good Philippe Beaumont."

Béchard noted this information, then produced a copy of the artist's rendition of the stalker. "Do you recognize this man?"

"*Ah, non. Je regrette /* Sorry."

"Perhaps we should be going now," Béchard said as he rose. "We have taken up enough of your time."

"Yes," I added. "You have been so kind to speak with us. We don't want to tire you out."

Henri didn't protest. He said good-bye from his chair and let us see ourselves to the door.

I glanced back and saw he was nodding off. We slipped out the door and down the stairs, eager to discuss all we had just learned.

# Chapter 31

On the sidewalk, Béchard asked, "Shall we go someplace to discuss Henri's revelations?"

"Absolutely. Can we walk for bit? I could use some air. That apartment was hot and stuffy. The wine went to my head."

"*Pas de problem* / no problem. Let us visit the Jardin du Luxembourg. It is such a beautiful park. My favorite in all of Paris."

"Sounds good. Which way?"

Within minutes, we entered the park, a large French-style garden. Flowers of every size, shape and color bordered expanses of finely-manicured lawns. Gravel alleys wound their way around an abundance of statuary and the occasional pond. In another reality I might have found the setting calm and relaxing. Today, it was nothing but a blur.

"What do you think about everything we learned from Henri?" I asked.

"Interesting." He indicated our route, a path surrounding a rectangle of lawn bordered by pink and purple flowers.

"Interesting? Is that all you can say? Don't you ever get excited? The man gave us all kinds of new leads." I bit my lip to avoid saying more, then quickened my step to keep up with Béchard. His legs were longer than mine.

He gave me a wry look. "It was *most* interesting. And you are correct. We now have additional information. But what have we actually learned?"

I didn't need time to think. "Solange, for one thing. Her connection to Marie. That was a surprise. I wonder why Marie never mentioned it to me."

Béchard shrugged. "Perhaps she felt it was not your business to know this. But does this relationship also connect her to the note? Or to the traitor?"

"Not necessarily." I frowned as I considered some possibilities. "Do you think Solange might be the missing link?"

"A link to the past, *absolument* / absolutely. But not a suspect. I see no motive for her to kill Toussaint, Moreau or Marie."

I couldn't argue.

"Let us not confuse ourselves by over-complicating the issue," he continued. "It has been my experience that the most common motives for murder tend to be the most simple, the most basic. We should examine the obvious first."

"And what, or whom, do you consider obvious?"

"I have no confirmed suspicions at this time, but let us approach this logically. Bear in mind that the traitor would be approximately the same age as Renoud, Henri and Marie. It is doubtful he would be capable of committing a violent murder."

"He may have an accomplice. Someone younger. Like my tattooed stalker."

"A missing link?" He raised his eyebrows.

"Are you mocking me?"

"A little. But that doesn't mean I don't take what you say quite seriously."

I laughed. "That sounds like police jargon to me. What about this Pecheur that Henri mentioned? The man was involved in the Résistance. Doesn't his name strike you as a coincidence since Marie's last word was 'peche'?"

"Perhaps. However, let us not forget that according to Henri this man left France many years ago. He changed his identity. It seems unlikely he should now be involved in recent deaths in Paris."

"You're probably right. But Henri also said that Pecheur has a son. He may be in Paris. Could he be the man with the red tattoo?"

"Pecheur's son would be at least 30 years older than your tattooed stalker. Pecheur left France toward the end of the Occupation. Katya was pregnant at this time. Mathematics disprove your theory." He consulted his watch. "It is nearly 4:30. Early for dinner by Parisian standards. Nevertheless, I am hungry. I neglected to eat lunch today."

My stomach agreed. "Me too. What did you have in mind?"

"A seafood restaurant in the Place St. Sulpice, across from the church, has an excellent reputation. I have been wanting to try it. If you do not object to being perhaps the only customers, I believe I can offer you an excellent dining experience."

*Were we going on a date? No, probably not. More like a business meeting*. "Which way?"

As we walked toward an exit to the park, I noticed a large poster advertising a puppet theater up the way and off to the left. "Puppets," I said, talking to myself.

"*Comment*? / What did you say?"

"I said 'puppets'."

He glanced at the poster. "Do you wish to visit the puppet theater?"

"No. But a puppet may provide the answer. Or at least part of it. Instead of a missing link, we may be looking for a puppeteer controlling the action. And a puppet carrying it out."

Béchard stared at me.

I continued. "As you said, our current suspects are too old to be committing violent murders. And Tattoo is too young to be

Pecheur's son. Perhaps the guilty party is using somebody else, somebody unrelated to anything, to do the deed for him. Somebody like my tattooed stalker."

"Are you suggesting a hired killer?"

"Why not?"

"Once again you present a factor which complicates rather than simplifies the situation."

No point arguing. "Just a thought."

We reached the Place St. Sulpice in a matter of minutes. The restaurant, La Méditeranée, was an attractive spot, sporting blue and white striped awnings and plenty of outdoor seating.

"Do you prefer to dine indoors or in the fresh air?" he asked.

"It's too nice a day to stay inside."

A waiter led us to a sidewalk table with a lovely view of the square. I peered through the window and saw we were not the only early diners. A family of four, most likely tourists, was well into their meal. Relieved to have something mundane to do, I studied the menu.

Béchard began to speak, but stopped short as I started laughing. "What is funny?"

I giggled a bit more. "It's the English translation on the menu." I pointed to an item marked 'Pork Shops.' "One letter can change so much."

He nodded, but didn't join in my laughter. "I believe I will have the *truite* / trout."

"I'll have Coquilles St. Jacques."

Béchard summoned the waiter and placed our order, including a bottle of Vouvray.

"Peche," I said aloud. I'd been talking to myself a lot lately. Bad habit. "One accent can change a lot as well."

"I beg your pardon?"

"I said 'peche'. Marie's last word, as well as your choice for dinner."

He rolled his eyes.

"Think about the word, like we discussed yesterday," I said. "I know the French don't pay much attention to accent marks nowadays, but when I was in school, my teacher was manic about them. She stressed the fact that a change in an accent mark sometimes changes the entire meaning of a word."

Béchard put down his fork and gave me his full attention.

"If you write 'peche' with an *accent circonflexe*, it means 'peach'. Change that to an *accent aigu* and it means 'sin'. We won't even talk about what happens when you start conjugating the verbs 'to sin' and 'to fish' and sometimes need an *accent grave*."

"Are you now wondering which accent mark Marie was using with her dying breath?"

"It's worth considering."

"An interesting line of conjecture. Unfortunately, I cannot imagine how this idea may lead us to the truth. Not only that, but 'peche' may be only a portion of a word. Consider 'dépêche' or 'empêche' for example."

"Or Pecheur." I sat back to watch for his reaction.

He smiled. "With or without a capital P?"

"I beg your pardon?"

"With a capital, it could be Henri's friend Jean-Paul. With a small p, it would be a fisherman, or a sinner."

"Good point."

The waiter appeared with our meals. My Coquilles St. Jacques—scallops in a rich cream sauce topped with cheese and served in a coquille shell—was delicious. I watched Béchard attack his trout. It was served European style, head and all, lying on the plate looking up at him. He decapitated and deboned it expertly, then dug in. We ate in silence.

Finishing the last of his meal, Béchard took out his notebook and began to write.

"Always working, aren't you?" I regretted my words immediately. It sounded petulant, as if I were disappointed he was more interested in business than in me. That was not so. We were having a business dinner, not a date. And I was thinking about the issues at hand every bit as hard as he was working making notes.

He looked up from his notebook. "There are many things I must attend to tomorrow. It helps to prepare a list."

"What's on your agenda?"

"The report of Moreau's death should have arrived by now. Also any information we can find on his telephone records. There is our missing copy of the note to locate, and…" he scanned his notes, "the son of Jean-Paul Pecheur and Katya Beaumont. From what Henri said, our files may contain information concerning this individual. What will you do with your day?"

"Return to the dig. After all, I am volunteering there. I'd like to speak with Claude again, as well as anybody else who feels like chatting. I'm not sure what I'm hoping to hear, but if I hang around and make idle conversation, I may learn something of value."

"Do you feel safe doing this?"

"I think so. After all, I no longer have a copy of the note. What else could someone want from me?"

# Chapter 32

I overslept the next morning. Gulping down a quick cup of coffee, I donned my digging attire—cut-off jeans, Star Trek T-shirt and sneakers—and prepared to head to St. Denis.

My cell phone rang as I bounded down the stairs.

"*Ah, Mademoiselle*, I am most relieved to find you at home."

"Who is this?" Definitely not Béchard. Who else in Paris had my number?

"Jean Renoud."

I had forgotten that Béchard gave him my number. It was early in the day for Renoud to be drinking, but his voice was unsteady.

"Are you all right?" I asked.

"It is urgent that I see you. You must come here at once. Please."

"Has something happened?"

"Not yet, but it will. And soon. Please come quickly."

"I don't understand."

"You will. I am in Versailles. You must come here now." He slurred these last words.

"What are you doing in Versailles?"

"Hiding. At the home of an old friend. My life is in danger."

The man was definitely drunk. He was also terrified.

"Tell me what has happened. If you're in danger, you should speak with *Inspecteur* Béchard. He'd be much better able to help you than I would."

"Béchard is not available. I cannot wait. And I will not keep this thing with me. You must come now, to the *Hameau* at Versailles. I will meet you there."

"What thing?" *And what the hell was the Hameau*?

His voice fell to a whisper. "The traitor's note. The original. It arrived in the morning post. Marie mailed it to me the night of her death."

A chill ran up my back. A message from a dead woman. No wonder the poor man was upset. "Did she include a note to you?"

"*Oui, Mademoiselle*." Renoud's voice shook. His tears were audible. "She said she dared not keep the note. Toussaint and Moreau once had it in their possession. They were both murdered. Marie feared for her life as well. She believed I would know what to do with it. But I don't. Come to the *Hameau*. If I am not there, it will mean it was not safe for me to wait. In that case, I will tape an envelope under the bench by the spiral stairway. It is easy to locate. There is only one such stairway. Hurry, please."

I had no good response to his plea. I listened as he broke down completely, sobbing into the phone. I took a deep breath and organized my thoughts. "I will contact Inspecteur Béchard. We will be there as soon as possible."

I rummaged in my bag for Béchard's number. The first two times I dialed the station, I got voicemail. The third attempt produced a live person.

"*Inspecteur Béchard, s'il vous plaît*."

"*Je regrette* / I am sorry, he is in conference and cannot be disturbed. Please call later."

"This is an emergency."

"*Je regrette. C'est impossible.*"

Damn French bureaucracy! I left an urgent message saying I was headed to the *Hameau* at Versailles and that it was critical for him to meet me there as quickly as possible. Renoud's life was in danger.

My head pounded as I disconnected the call. No time to call the dig to inform them I wouldn't be coming. I got directions to Versailles from my landlady and dashed up the street.

In the Métro car, I caught my breath and considered the situation. Renoud's fears were not groundless. If his phone had been tapped as Marie's had been, somebody could know he had the original note. That didn't matter now. What did matter was calming the man down and retrieving the note from him. Béchard and I could deal with it.

I exited the train at Châtelet Station and entered the dreary tunnel which would take me to the connecting line for St. Lazare. The station was eerily quiet this morning, and nearly deserted. I found myself alone in the tunnel. And not at all comfortable. The lighting was poor, the air cool and damp. And not a sound to be heard. The hairs on my neck prickled. Taking long slow breaths, I tried to pretend everything was fine. It didn't work.

I heard somebody approaching me. Walking quickly. Now directly behind me. I stepped to the right to allow whoever it was to pass. A brown-skinned man wearing a bright red jacket walked by me, then stopped short and turned, blocking my way.

I was in trouble. I held my breath and tried to walk past him.

He had other ideas.

He grabbed me by the belt.

I swung around and faced him.

"*Donnez-moi le sac* / Give me your bag," he ordered. With his free hand, he produced a knife, flashing it at me as he repeated, "*Donnez-moi le sac*."

Son of a bitch! I was being mugged.

Time stood still, just like in the movies. Sounds echoed off the walls. Rage welled up within me. No way in hell would I be this thug's victim. I spun to the right with all my might, releasing my assailant's grip on me. Muscle memory kicked in as I remembered some fencing moves Pete had taught me. I parried, stepping back a few feet, so my assailant couldn't reach me, then lunged toward him. I swung my shoulder bag low and under his knife, then flung it up with all the force I could muster. My attack took him by surprise. He dropped the knife, giving me the time I needed to break into a run.

I ran at warp two, shouting "Help, help." Then I remembered I was in France. "Help" wouldn't work. I changed my cries to "Police"—the same word in both French and English.

Panting, I turned to see if the mugger was behind me. He was. And he was gaining on me. I ran even faster, screamed even louder. Arriving at a flight of stairs, I mounted them two at a time. Somehow, I made it to the top.

I stopped, looked back. No sign of my assailant. In front of me were at least 20 people waiting for the train. Nobody looked my way.

"*Quelqu'un vient de m'attaquer en bas* / Somebody just attacked me down there," I shouted. That got everybody's attention. Two men rushed at me. Their clothing and hair made them look like aging hippies. Were they going to mug me as well?

I needn't have worried. The first to reach me flashed a badge in my face. "*Police*." They were undercover cops.

Relief surged through my veins. This was the first time in my life I had ever screamed for the police, and their arrival was almost instantaneous. The two of them questioned me.

"What did he look like?"

"What was he wearing?"

"Did he harm you?"

"Did he take anything?"

"Which way did he go?"

I answered as best I could—in French, in English, in pantomime. I couldn't remember the French word for jacket. Somehow, they understood me.

One officer dashed down the stairs and into the tunnel. The other remained long enough to tell me to stay put, then disappeared down the stairs as well.

I was alone, but in a crowd, and out of immediate danger. My adrenaline level returned closer to normal. Then my legs, which only moments ago had served me so well, turned to jello. I collapsed onto a bench. A train arrived and was quickly boarded by everybody on the platform. I was alone again.

The sound of sirens assaulted my ears, that awful Gestapo-like sound French sirens make. How long had they been blaring like that? The noise stopped suddenly, and two uniformed policemen approached me on the platform. I ran to join them.

The two undercover cops returned at the same time, unsuccessful in catching my assailant. They conferred with the newly-arrived officers, then went back down the stairs. The uniformed officers questioned me, taking notes as they did.

"Please," I said to them, "do you know *Inspecteur* Paul Béchard? It is critical that I speak with him immediately. We are working on a case together. I have important news for him. Please contact him at once." No point spelling it out for them. The details would take too long.

A cop punched some numbers into his phone. After a brief conversation, he said, "Béchard is unavailable at the moment."

"Then please give him a message for me. Tell him to get to Versailles as quickly as possible. To meet me in the *Hameau*. Renoud is there. He has the note. His life is in danger."

One of the officers opened his mouth to speak when his phone rang. He had a brief conversation, then rang off. "*Mademoiselle,* we must respond to an emergency. Please go to the Préfecture at once and file a report. Perhaps you may speak with *Inspecteur* Béchard while you are there."

And they were gone.

I stood alone on the sidewalk taking deep breaths and scanning the area for anybody who looked suspicious. The problem was everybody did. Where the hell was Béchard when I needed him? And where could I get a train to Versailles?

# Chapter 33

# Judas

At last! They were finally getting somewhere. And for once, Philippe's criminal friends had proven helpful. They tapped Renoud's phone. It paid off. They heard him speaking with the American bitch, planning to meet her at Versailles.

Renoud, of all people. Renoud, who had disappeared so many years ago, after Marie's arrest. He had the note, the original, and was afraid to keep it. As much a coward as ever.

The nosy American was going to get the note from Renoud.

Even Philippe couldn't mess it up now. All he had to do was follow this bitch and get the note from her. By any means necessary. She was expendable.

Soon he would be safe.

# Chapter 34

As the train pulled into Versailles, my heart in my mouth, I followed the crowds of tourists up the street, then stopped dead as the palace came into view. I had expected big; this was beyond enormous. A gilded gate adorned the entrance to Versailles. The palace was everywhere I looked, with wings longer than city blocks extending on both sides.

Standing on the cobblestones, I stared into the courtyard. Now what? Congratulations Amy. You've done it again. Set yourself up for God knows what. Why didn't you hide in your room and wait for Béchard? Had to be the hero didn't you?

Hoping for a few moments of safety, I inserted myself into the middle of a group of Japanese tourists. A few of them looked my way. I forced a smile. This was good. I fit right in, height-wise anyway.

A sign announced that the palace itself was closed on Mondays. Visitors were, however, welcome to explore the formal gardens and the *Hameau*. An arrow pointed the way through the open courtyard to the rear of the palace. My Asian protectors headed straight for the formal gardens. I tried to will them to go to the *Hameau* instead; it didn't work.

I grabbed a brochure and scanned it. The "*Hameau*" was described as a small hamlet in the woods built for Marie

Antoinette so she could play at being a peasant. It was good to be queen. Not so good to be heading into the woods alone.

I was on the verge of a minor panic attack when my phone rang. Hopefully Béchard calling to tell me he'd arrive any second.

"*C'est moi*, Amy. I have been informed of your recent attack, and of your plans to go to Versailles. Most unwise."

"I'm in Versailles now. Where are you? Will you be here soon?"

"*Du calme*," he said. "Please tell me what has happened."

"I called you earlier this morning. You were in a conference. They refused to interrupt you. And this was urgent. It still is."

"What is urgent?"

I took a long, deep breath. "Renoud phoned me. Terrified. He received a piece of mail—from Marie."

"*Comment?* / What?"

"She sent him the note. The original. She must have posted it shortly before she was attacked. She told him she didn't feel safe keeping it. Renoud doesn't feel safe with it either. He's convinced that if he has this cursed note he'll be killed like Toussaint and Marie and Moreau. He wants to meet us in the *Hameau* at Versailles to give us the note. When I couldn't contact you, I came here by myself to get it from him. So he wouldn't do anything foolish."

"You decided to do something foolish yourself instead. You should have come directly to the Préfecture as instructed, to report your attack rather than place yourself in danger."

"It's too late for that. Please tell me you'll be here soon."

"I shall not be long. I am concluding urgent business which could not wait."

"Isn't this note urgent business as well?" *Never mind my own safety.*

Béchard hesitated. "I did not wish to tell you this, preferring not to add to your worries at the moment."

"What? Has something else happened?"

"Claude, from the dig, was found dead this morning, in his apartment."

Son of a bitch! Him too! "How did it happen?"

"He was hanged."

"Do you mean he killed himself?"

"We cannot be sure. I am at the scene now. We should finish here shortly."

What was I supposed to do in the meantime? Just loiter around Versailles? "Do you want me to get the note from Renoud and bring it to the local police station? Leave it for you there?"

"*Ah, non*, that may not be wise. With our copy already missing and my concerns about the possibility of a traitor within our ranks, I do not dare let more police officers know the original has been located. We cannot risk losing this as well."

"Then, what?" I struggled to control the anger in my voice. Or was it panic? Maybe both.

Béchard was silent for a moment. "Claude's apartment is near Versailles. I will conclude my business here as quickly as possible. Get the note from Renoud and wait for me in the *Hameau*. It's a tourist attraction; there will be plenty of people around. Please remain with the crowd until I arrive."

I steeled myself and forged on in the direction of the *Hameau*. My only solace was that a mass of tourists was walking in the same direction.

Struggling to appear nonchalant, I caught up with a group of six people speaking German. Pushing past the first four, I joined the two in the lead. They moved to the right to let me pass. I kept pace with them instead. They gave me an odd look, but said nothing. Together we continued to the end of the path.

I jumped as a loud noise reached my ears. It sounded like a gunshot. *But no*, I told myself. *That couldn't be. Not here. Not in a crowded tourist attraction.*

A sign announced the "*Hameau de la Reine*," a little village of cottages with thatched roofs and ivy climbing up their sides. A charming spot. Or it would have been if Renoud's life weren't in danger.

My eyes wandered around the hamlet in search of Renoud. I pushed my fears out of my mind. It was important to appear calm when I saw him. The man had been so upset on the phone. No point making it worse.

Renoud was pacing in front of a rose-covered cottage. He ran to join me, stumbling, nearly falling, on the way. And no small wonder. He reeked of liquor. I couldn't blame the poor old soul.

"*Mademoiselle*," he whispered, "we must be most careful not to attract attention. Not to be seen together. I am going to walk to the rear of this cottage. Do not come with me, but join me there in a few moments."

I did as instructed. We were alone behind the cottage, hidden from view.

Pulling an envelope from a dusty old leather satchel, he thrust it toward me. "It is most urgent that you deliver this to the police at once."

"I will do that. *Inspecteur* Béchard will be here any minute."

"You are very kind to an old man. *Merci*."

"I'm happy to help. Think of it as my way of thanking you for the work you did during the Occupation."

He nodded, eyes wide, face pale.

"No harm will come to you now," I told him, hoping it wasn't a lie. "You must be brave."

"I am not a brave man, *Mademoiselle*."

"Do it for Marie. For her memory. Remember, this was important to her."

He nodded and sped off into the woods. Then I heard that sound again, coming from the direction that Renoud had taken. Definitely a gunshot. Had they killed Renoud as well? My blood pressure soared and my hands shook as I gazed at the paper he had given me, my vision blurred with unshed tears. Would I be next? And where the Hell was Béchard? No amount of yoga breathing could help me now. I was on the verge of a full-blown panic attack.

Not knowing how else to proceed, I folded the envelope containing the infamous note and crammed it into the makeup kit in my shoulder bag to keep the note safe while I waited. I willed Béchard to hurry.

The cottage closest to me, with pink and purple flowers blooming on the porch, had two wooden benches, both unoccupied. A reasonable spot to watch for Béchard. A group of people standing in front of the first bench protected me from the view of anybody approaching. At least for the moment.

I sat and looked around. To the right, a spiral wooden staircase covered with white and yellow flowers led to the upper level of the house. Beyond that was a small stone bridge. Just before the bridge was a dirt path. To the left was the gravel walkway by which I had arrived. I gazed in that direction. Surely Béchard would arrive from there. And then I gasped.

Tattoo was walking toward me, phone in hand. Slowly. He didn't pull out a gun or run at me. He simply glared and continued walking and talking on his phone.

My heart pounding and my head reeling, I did the only thing I could think of to protect myself. I rose from the bench, pointed at Tattoo and shrieked, "This man is trying to kill me!"

All heads turned in my direction.

"Help me, please! Don't let him near me! Don't let him kill me!" My voice began to crack as I sought refuge in the mass of tourists.

"*Du calme! Du calme*!" Tattoo shouted at the crowd as he pocketed his phone. "My wife is not well, *vous voyez* / you see. She neglected to take her medication this morning. I must bring her home to attend to her needs."

Apparently people believed him. Nobody came to my rescue as he grasped me by the arm and led me away, dragging me into a leaf-covered tunnel-like structure. It was at least twenty feet long, the interior dark. The leaves on the roof kept out the sunlight.

I closed my eyes, held my breath and prepared to meet my fate.

# Chapter 35

A man in a brown business suit entered the bower from an opening mid-way through. He held a gun, pointed directly at me.

Neither man spoke as Brown Suit grabbed my arm with his free hand and jerked me away from Tattoo, who then exited the bower, phone in hand. Brown Suit held me close enough that I could smell his cheap cologne. My shoulder bag banged sharply against my hip, a cruel reminder of what it held, as he pushed me through the bower.

Who the hell was this thug? I had never seen him before. And in that ugly brown suit, he would have stuck out like a sore thumb in the *Hameau*. Had he been following me as well?

My left arm hurt where he gripped it. A tear ran down my cheek. There was no escaping now. I was as dead as the others.

My captor jabbed his gun into my side. "You will be quiet, *Mademoiselle*. Or I shall be forced to shoot you."

"You won't shoot me here. Too many people around. Somebody would hear the shot."

"Perhaps not," he hissed at me. "Do you hear that sound?"

I listened for a moment. Gunshots.

He gave me an evil grin. "There is a shooting range nearby. One hears gunfire all the time. One shot more or less will alarm no one."

It was useless to struggle. I was trapped, unable to fight, or run, or even scream. This guy was taller than me by at least a foot. And a good deal stronger. The only solution was to outwit him. But how?

But they weren't going to kill me. Not here. Not yet. They wanted the blasted note. As long as I didn't give it to them, didn't tell them where it was, I had a chance. I'd play along for a while, be the good little victim until my brain came up with a plan. My wits had to keep me alive until Béchard showed up. When he didn't see me in the *Hameau*, he'd come looking for me. But how would he know where to look?

Tattoo interrupted my thoughts, walking toward me with a gun aimed at my heart. "*Eh bien*," he said to the other man, "let's get this over with."

Brown Suit grunted, poked me again with his gun and pushed me toward the other end of the bower.

Squinting as I was shoved into the sunlight, I looked around for anything that might help me escape. To the left was a building, apparently part of the hamlet, undergoing repair. It was fenced off from the rest of the area. No workmen there at the moment. Piles of lumber lying around. Nothing helpful in that direction.

Straight ahead on the path stood a wooden gate. It was open and led to a road. To the right, a ditch separated the hamlet grounds from the road.

Tattoo lagged behind, once again on his phone. Then he hurried to rejoin us. "There will be a slight delay. We will wait over there." He pointed to the pile of lumber.

His accomplice acknowledged this wordlessly, shoving me toward the lumber while jabbing the gun into my side. His other arm grasped me, nearly cutting off my circulation.

As we reached the construction materials, Tattoo stopped once more to use his phone. Brown Suit indicated I should get down on the ground behind the lumber.

Pretending to obey, I began to lower myself, then lunged forward butting my head into Brown Suit's chest, catching him off guard. He lurched, face first, into the lumber, dropping his gun as he fell.

Prepared for this, my one and only chance, I jumped up and ran to the gate. I was almost there when a shot rang out behind me. I ducked. Another shot. Still running, I ducked once more, then lost my footing and fell into the ditch. I hit bottom with a thud and a splash.

There I was, sprawled at the bottom of the muddy ditch, soaking wet, my shoulder bag hanging from my neck and down my back. I moved the bag to my side to prevent the strap from choking me.

Forcing myself to stand, I searched for a way to get out of the ditch. No luck.

"Do not move, *Mademoiselle*."

I looked up to find Tattoo standing by the ditch, threatening me with his gun. Brown Suit was nowhere in sight.

"Stay where you are," Tattoo ordered.

Standing in the ditch, wet and muddy, I wondered if I had just played out my last hand.

Tattoo stood guard, his eyes darting everywhere, the gun always trained on me. He shifted from one foot to the other. After a while he muttered, "*Enfin* / finally."

I followed his gaze to the road on the other side of the ditch. A car was approaching. It was large and black. I didn't recognize the make, nor could I see the plate. Tattoo motioned to the driver, indicating my location in the ditch. The car pulled up. The driver jumped out. Brown Suit appeared at the same time. Between the two of them, they hauled me out, soaked and muddy, nearly disconnecting my arms in the process.

Tattoo faced me, pistol in hand. "Give me the note."

"What note?"

"Do not play games with me. Give me the note."

"Then what?"

"Then I will shoot you."

I stood my ground. If they wanted the damn note, let them work for it. "I don't have it," I lied.

"Renoud gave it to you."

"No he didn't. He hid the note. He told me where to find it."

"Search her," Tattoo ordered the others.

Brown suit patted me down. The driver grabbed my shoulder bag and emptied it onto the ground. My only recourse now was to pray for a miracle. I held my breath as the driver pored through my belongings on the ground.

And it wasn't there! The make-up case where I had stashed the note wasn't in my bag. It must have fallen out at the bottom of the ditch. "I told you I didn't have it."

Tattoo scowled and shoved me into the back seat of the car. Brown Suit joined me. Tattoo rode shotgun, literally. The driver jumped in and we sped off.

No point in struggling. I was caught. For the moment, anyway. Might as well try to learn something. I sat back in the now-soggy seat. "Where are you taking me?"

No response.

"What are you going to do to me?

Again, no response.

"I'd like to know what's going on."

Tattoo spoke up. "*Mademoiselle*, you will be silent. You will know soon enough where we are going, and why. You have caused enough trouble for one day."

I started to close my eyes to shut it all out, then realized that was a bad idea. Better to pay attention to the road. In case I got a chance to get away. Hope was still springing eternal.

We were on a major highway, moving at an amazing speed. The signs indicated we were heading toward the Bois de Boulogne, the forest west of Paris.

These men were rank amateurs. They didn't blindfold me, or put me in the trunk, or even on the floor. They allowed me to see where we were going. That made no sense—unless they did intend to kill me.

That idea didn't set well. I was damned if I'd die over an old note. That may have been the fate of everybody else who had a copy of it. I wouldn't let it happen to me.

It dawned on me that there was a copy of the note in the claim file back in Boston. Nancy had seen it, and she was unharmed, so far.

Then a lightbulb went off in my head.

Nancy wasn't the only one in the office who had seen the note. My fax containing it had been misdirected when it arrived, sent to somebody else with the same last name—Nancy's father-in-law, CEO and president of NEC&I, J.P. Fisher. And Fisher in French is Pecheur! J.P. Fisher. Jean-Paul Pecheur. The same person? It made some sense. The age was about right. And it wasn't long after the fax was delivered to the old man that my troubles began over here. And I was taken off the case. It wasn't Mitch's doing. He was following orders. Fisher was Jean-Paul Pecheur. He was the traitor. He was orchestrating everything.

Son of a bitch! That had to be it! Now that I knew the truth, what was I going to do about it? What was I able to do?

At the speed we were moving, it didn't take long to reach Paris. We approached the Porte Maillot then cut across the Boulevard Périphérique. The Arc de Triomphe was dead ahead.

The driver took a sharp left and wove through a maze of side streets. I saw signs for the Gare St. Lazare, where I had caught the train for Versailles. I noted every street sign I could.

A short way up the rue de Madrid, the car stopped. It was a quiet street, apparently residential. We were in front of number 20.

"*Allons* / Let's go," Tattoo ordered. Brown Suit forced me onto the sidewalk. The car took off with a squeal of rubber.

For a brief moment I stood muddy and damp on the sidewalk before being ushered into the foyer. The two men placed themselves between me and the concierge, who communicated with the world through a window on the left side of the foyer. They lowered their guns as we passed.

"*Bonjour, Madame.*" Tattoo smiled at the woman. "We are going to visit *Monsieur* Beaumont. He is expecting us."

"*Ah, oui, oui*. He told me you would be coming."

I was pushed into a tiny elevator which looked to be at least fifty years old. *Beaumont*, *Beaumont*. I had heard that name before, and recently. I searched my memory banks.

Catherine Beaumont! Pecheur's lover. Renoud said they had a son. Was it Fisher's son I was now on my way to meet?

# Chapter 36

# Judas

Judas had mixed feelings as he gazed out the window of the plane—seeing nothing but the night.

He was returning to France, the country of his birth, the country he had vowed never again to visit. It was too dangerous. Or so he had always thought.

Now he was going there to eliminate the danger, having faced the unfortunate truth that he dared not trust things to his son Philippe. Judas had to be there, to see for himself that all was set right. He had to know, to feel, that he was out of danger. He needed to know that the note was destroyed, that the American bitch was silenced and that he need never again worry about the bastards finding him. His life lay in the balance.

Judas would actually meet Philippe, the son he had supported in luxury all these years, Catherine's son. First they had corresponded, lately they had spoken. To meet him face to face should prove interesting.

For years, he had been disappointed in his son. The boy was a petty crook, not smart enough to avoid being caught. Philippe had been quick to jump to his father's aid, to do everything in his power to ensure the man's safety. He was willing. That was certain. What Judas didn't know was: was his son capable?

He gazed out the window, wondering what awaited him upon the homecoming he never thought he would have.

# Chapter 37

The three of us squeezed into the elevator. Brown Suit jabbed his gun into my ribs. I got the message and stayed on my best behavior. The man reeked of sweat and Gauloise cigarettes, nauseating me in the cramped quarters.

Tattoo closed the elevator door and pressed a button. The elevator moved at a shaky snail's pace. Nobody spoke.

The uncomfortable ride ended. We exited. They pushed me to the left. A door swung open and a middle-aged man ushered us inside. Brown Suit shoved me into a room on the right and deposited me onto a chair in front of a fireplace. He rejoined the other two men in the entryway but kept his eyes, and his gun, on me as they conferred.

I couldn't hear what they were saying. It was probably just as well. I needed to calm myself and shove my fears aside so I could come up with a way out of this mess. No way I wanted my life to end in Beaumont's living room. I concentrated on studying my surroundings.

An apartment. The room where I sat, quite possibly waiting to die, was filled with formal, expensive-looking furniture. The chairs by the fireplace were trimmed in gold. Would they shoot me here and get my blood all over these nice furnishings? Probably. They had left me here caked in mud.

The glass-topped coffee table in front of me was modern and out-of-sync with the other furnishings. It was strewn with newspapers, dirty paper cups and glasses, and a messy pile of scrawled notes. I strained to read the notes when I heard movement to my left.

"We'll return in an hour," Brown Suit said. I turned to see him and Tattoo slip out the door, relieved to know they wouldn't be waiting in the hallway to foil any possible escape I might attempt.

Beaumont now held the gun. He walked toward me. His navy blue suit looked expensive, as did his red silk tie and black leather shoes. I examined his face. He bore a sharp resemblance to J.P. Fisher. Same small dark eyes, thin lips, square jaw, same sour scowl. No doubt in my mind he was Fisher's son.

It was just the two of us now. I had to out-think the man or I'd be dead.

He sat across the coffee table from me and fondled his weapon. "*Eh bien, Mademoiselle*, you have succeeded in making a great nuisance of yourself. That is ended. There will be no more trouble. Give me the note."

"What note is that?" I worked on being coy, didn't quite pull it off.

"No games. You have the note." His voice hardened. "Give it to me now."

"I don't have it."

"But you know where it is. You will tell me."

He was every bit as bossy as his father. "And then what?"

"Then you die."

I folded my hands in my lap to hide the fact that they were shaking. "If that's the case, *Monsieur* Beaumont, I would like to know what I'm dying for. What is this all about? Why is this note so important to your father, Jean-Paul Pecheur?" I'd question him ad nauseum if it would keep him from shooting me.

"So you know my father's name. What else do you know?"

"Just that this old note is important to him. Why do you want it so badly?"

"To save a hero who has been falsely accused. To protect him."

"Your father wasn't a hero. He was a traitor."

Beaumont scowled. "*Ah non*, he was not a traitor. That note is full of lies—created by the true traitor in an effort to save himself by casting suspicion on my father. My father was a hero who was forced to flee, to leave my mother, never to return, all because of the lies in that note. It is vital that I destroy all copies of it to prevent it from falling into the wrong hands. Even now, after so many years, those lies would ruin him."

He stared at me, his gun aimed straight at my heart.

"Your mother was Catherine Beaumont."

His face softened. "They called her Katya, a nickname from the old days. But to my father, she was always Catherine."

"I've heard of Katya. She was in the same Résistance cell as Pecheur."

"*Ah, oui*, she worked alongside my father, the love of her life. Until the lies began and he was forced to escape. She was pregnant with me, but hid this from him. So great was her love for him she was willing to raise me alone to save his life. She would not allow me to take his name, fearing this might expose one or both of us to danger. Always protecting those she loved."

The gun lay limply in his lap now. This was good. I had to keep him talking. "She must have been an amazing woman."

"Amazing, extraordinary, loving, beautiful, all those things and more. And strong, very strong. She was deserving of my father's love."

"She never saw him again?"

"*Hélas, non*."

"But she knew where he was."

"*Ah, non.* That knowledge would have been too dangerous. It was better that we never knew where he was."

"But they were able to communicate."

"Ma*is oui.* At first, through that fool Henri. He passed messages between them when my father first escaped. Later, when my father was settled and had established a new identity, their communication was through Moreau. It was safer that way. Henri could not be trusted with the knowledge of my father's new identity, or his whereabouts. He would have betrayed him out of stupidity. Moreau was better, more devoted to my father. Moreau would do anything to help my father, to keep him safe."

"So your father kept in contact with you and your mother through Moreau? And learned of your birth through him? "

"And sent us money, lots of money. My father became a very wealthy man. My mother never wanted for anything. He gave her a good life. And me as well. Even after my mother died, he continued to support me, to communicate with me through Moreau. Then Moreau betrayed him. Betrayed the man he had worshipped for so long, the hero he had protected. It was unforgivable the way Moreau turned on my father."

Beaumont's scowl tightened. So did his grip on the gun.

"How did Moreau betray him?"

"When he decoded the note, he believed the lies it contained. How could he? He who knew my father so well. Such a fool he was in the end. He was going to spread the lies and destroy my father. I couldn't let that happen."

He paused, as if lost in thought. A brief smile passed over his face. "My father telephoned me. For the first time I my life, I spoke directly with him. I heard his voice. He was in danger. He required my assistance. My assistance! All my life he had provided for me. I now saw the chance to repay him in a small way."

Some small way. Killing so many people. I was dealing with a madman. "So you went to see Moreau after your father's call. And you killed him."

"It was necessary, and not at all difficult. Moreau was a feeble old man. He trusted me. The fool thought I, too, would believe the lies in the note. He showed me a copy of it without hesitation. He actually expected me to commiserate with him about being betrayed. As if my father was capable of such betrayal. *Non.* My father was a hero. He saved many lives. Moreau's lack of faith cost him his life."

"How did you disguise the fact that he was murdered?"

Beaumont sat up a bit straighter, his chest puffed out. "I suffocated him with a pillow and left him on his bed. It would appear that his heart had given out. He was old and alone. Nobody would question his death."

That much was true. Nobody had questioned Moreau's death. "Did you murder Toussaint as well?"

He nodded. "It was unfortunate he was unwilling to cooperate. All I really wanted from him was the note. The original and any copies. It could have been simple. If he had given me the note before it was decoded, I may have let him live."

"Why did you kill him?"

"I did not intend to do so." Beaumont sighed. "I telephoned him, posing as Moreau's son. I informed him that my alleged father had information for him concerning the note, but had taken ill and was unable to speak with him in person. I was to act as messenger. Toussaint agreed to meet me that evening at a café in St. Denis. I told him there was a small problem with the copy of the note. The photocopy quality was poor, making certain parts unreadable. I told him my father must have the original in order to decode it."

"But he didn't give it to you."

"He said he didn't have it. How was I to know he was telling the truth? The head archaeologist must surely have the original. I told myself he was lying. I pressed him on this. Apparently I pushed too hard and he became suspicious. He left the café saying he would find another way to get the note decoded."

I sat on the edge of my chair, almost afraid to hear what he'd say next.

Beaumont frowned. "I followed Toussaint into the street. We argued. He insisted he did not have the original. Said he'd given it to one of the senior archaeologists and was unsure how many copies were made. He walked away from me. I lost my temper. There was a pile of lumber on the sidewalk nearby, for work being done on a building. I grabbed a board, caught up behind the man and hit him on the head."

"How did Toussaint's body end up in the pit at the dig site?"

"It was necessary to hide the body as quickly as possible. Happily, there was no blood to leave a trail."

Happily? His sentiment appalled me.

"There was a wheelbarrow on the sidewalk nearby. I loaded the body into it. Toussaint's keys fell from his pocket as I did this. There was a padlock in the fence a little way up the street. It was not difficult to find the correct key. Once inside the site, I realized it was the perfect spot. How simple it would be to make it appear that Toussaint had an accident, that he fell into the pit when the plank slipped from its support on the side. I tossed his body into the pit, then pulled the plank loose and threw that in as well. Finally, I disturbed the earth where the plank had rested to make it appear that it had come loose and given way. Then I went off to locate the note."

"What about the other work site? Was it you who vandalized that?"

"*Oui*, for insurance."

Funny he should use that word.

"I destroyed the urn in which the note had been hidden. That way, there was less proof of its existence."

It was hard to follow his reasoning here. Had he destroyed the urn purely out of spite?

"Then I entered the office of the dig and searched for copies of the note."

"But you didn't find them."

"*Hélas, non.* I made a thorough search, but found nothing."

No wonder. Claude hadn't kept the copies of the note in his office. Claude thought like an archaeologist. The note was simply one of many items found at the dig site. He kept it with the other artifacts in that dingy front room overflowing with finds and organized into a system known to Claude alone.

"Then you began following Marie hoping to get the note that way."

"That part was easy."

"And you tapped her phone as well?"

"*Pourquoi pas* / Why not? I had associates with the means to do this. It was a logical way to proceed. It paid off quickly. Marie's call to Renoud informed me she was bringing the note to him. It was a simple matter to dispose of her *en route*."

"And you also had Claude killed." Might as well hear his full confession. And the longer I kept him talking, the longer I lived—maybe even long enough to find a way to escape.

"*Mais oui.* He refused to tell me where his copies were. Accused me of attempting to steal his precious 'finds' and claim them as my own. Such a fool. He had no idea of the true importance of, or the danger in, what he had."

"I suppose that murder was simple as well."

"*Bien sûr.* He, too, was an old man. No match for my strength. I overpowered him, then hanged him to make it appear a suicide."

I shuddered at how easily Beaumont discussed murder. And at the thought that I could be next. "Did your father tell you to have me followed as well? To have my room searched?"

Beaumont stiffened. He sat up straight and grasped the gun tightly. His mouth twitched. "Enough of this nonsense. What need is there for you to know? In a minute, you shall be dead. Now tell me where the note is hidden." He raised the gun and pointed it at me.

I swallowed my tears and faked bravado. "I hid it in the grounds of Versailles. If you kill me, you'll never find it. If you bring me there, I can show you where it is." And perhaps lead him into a crowd and find a way to escape.

A loud knock at the door interrupted his response.

Beaumont stood to answer it, keeping the gun on me as he moved toward the door.

"Philippe," an unseen voice ordered. "Let me in."

# Chapter 38

"Q*ui est-ce?* / Who is it?" Beaumont demanded as he approached the door.

"It is your father. Let me in at once."

"Papa?" His face lit up as he threw the door open. "Papa!"

This domestic scene provided me a welcome reprieve. I glanced around for a means of escape while Beaumont was distracted. It was no use. Beaumont's papa pushed past his astonished son and approached me, gun in hand.

"Hello, Mr. Fisher. What brings you to Paris?"

"Quite obviously, I have come to kill you." He sat in an armchair across the coffee table from me. Beaumont took the chair beside me, turned so he could keep his gun aimed at my heart.

I forced a smile. "Jean-Paul Pecheur, J.P. Fisher. Not a very original alias." *Might as well meet the man head-on. No point in dying a coward.*

He sneered. "It's your own fault. You should have taken a normal vacation like everybody else. Then you never would have become mixed up in this. Blame yourself, as well as that mealy-mouthed Nancy my other son married."

Beaumont's mouth fell open. "Your other son? You have another son?"

Fisher turned to Beaumont. "Yes, Philippe. You have a younger brother. We'll discuss that later."

Beaumont stared at his father, eyes wide.

I spoke up. "After you read the fax I sent Nancy, you decided to get rid of me. You had me followed. And my room searched."

Fisher said nothing, but kept the gun trained on me.

"Did you also arrange to have me mugged?"

Fisher turned to his son. "Well?"

"Sadly, that did not go as planned. The attack was premature. Mademoiselle Lynch did not yet have the note."

He didn't mention how cleverly I'd foiled my assailant.

And there they were, the newly-united father and son, each holding a gun on me. Nobody spoke for a moment.

Curiosity overcame me. I wanted the whole story. "So, Mr. Fisher, you were the traitor." It was a statement, not a question.

Beaumont jumped to his father's defense. "He was no traitor. He was a hero. The rest is all lies." He waved his gun in the air, his finger twitching on the trigger.

I held my breath.

Fisher glowered at his son. "You believed all that crap I fed your mother, *hein*? That I was doing something great and noble and needed her protection? You're as big a fool as she was." He sighed and shook his head.

"But you loved my mother! You wouldn't lie to her."

"Loved? Maybe. Enjoyed? Definitely. Needed? Badly. Oh yes, I required her protection, but for reasons far different than what you believe."

"*Non, Papa.* I cannot believe you were a traitor. I will not believe it." His lips quivered as he spoke.

Fisher silenced him. "Such a harsh word, traitor. One must not think of me in those terms. I was not a traitor. Nor was I a hero. I was an avenger. Nothing more, nothing less."

"*Comment*? / I do not understand."

But I understood all too well. "You betrayed the Résistance and turned innocent people over to the Nazis out of revenge?"

"They got nothing more than they deserved. They were not innocent. They were the enemy. They destroyed my father, my family. I could not let them destroy me as well. They had to pay. Pay with their lives and their fortunes."

"Who had to pay?" I asked. "And for what?"

"The Jews. After what they did to my father, the Jews had to pay." He grimaced. "My father had a small insurance company. Nothing grand, but we lived well. At the end of a year in which losses had been large and profits small, the bankers, the Jewish bankers, called in his loans. There was no reason for them to do so. The company would have recovered in time. The bankers were greedy. They wouldn't wait. My father lost the company, lost our home, lost it all."

He paused and glared at me. "After that, life became difficult. My father began to drink, then to drink more. He died soon after. The drinking killed him. That and the Jews who stole his life from him, stole his self-respect. My mother and I were left with nothing. I swore two things—that I would not live my life in poverty and that I would avenge my father's death."

Why was he telling us this? For my benefit? For Beaumont's? For his own? There was a dazed look in the man's eyes. I sat motionless as Pecheur continued his story.

"The war provided me with my opportunity. A minor lameness in my left leg exempted me from the fighting. When Paris became occupied, I secretly approached the Germans and volunteered my services. We agreed that I would find my way into an underground group working to smuggle Jews out of the country. Once I gained their trust, I would gradually turn more and more of these refugees over to the Germans. And they would pay me handsomely."

"So you joined up with Marie, Henri, Renoud and the others."

"*Oui*. How simple it was to win their confidence. How easily they believed my lies. It was almost amusing to watch their bewildered annoyance as so many of their plans went wrong."

"But they did suspect a traitor in their midst," I reminded him. "Marie told me so."

"Ah, Marie. The only one with half a brain. That made her dangerous. It became obvious I would have to eliminate her. But I was young then, sentimental. To kill such a charming young woman was more than I could bear. Instead, I arranged for the Germans to catch her smuggling forged passports and imprison her. That put her out of my way for a long time."

My spine shivered as I listened to him tell his story in such cold, clinical terms. "But after Marie was arrested, didn't the group break up?"

A nasty sneer appeared on his face. "You are well-informed, Ms. Lynch. I was able to join another group. Henri was helpful with this. In a short while, I resumed my double role, and became rich in the process. Not only did the Germans pay me, but the Jews as well. They gave me their fortunes, their jewels, all that they had. Anything for a chance at freedom, for a chance for life."

So that's where he got the money to start his own insurance company. And the antique bracelet he gave to Nancy. I cringed at the realization. My income all these years came from the proceeds of extortion, blood money.

Fisher continued his ramblings. "It eventually became obvious that the game was up. Once again the group began to have suspicions. Someone actually had me followed. It became dangerous for me to continue. I could not be discovered. I had seen what the Résistance did to those who betrayed them, how they had killed Antoine without hesitation. I had amassed a small fortune. Time to get out before my true role was discovered. So I wrote the note."

Beaumont's gasped. "You wrote the note? How can that be? You told me it was planted by those who wished to accuse you falsely, that it was filled with lies."

"You still don't get it, do you?" Fisher sneered at his son. "The note was a plea to my German friends to assist me in escaping, as they had promised to do. I encoded it, left it in my usual drop-site on the rue Jean Jaurès."

"In the urn." I added.

"Of course. Then the planes came and bombed the neighborhood. I barely got away in time. I thought the note was destroyed by the bombing and searched for another means of escape. My good friend Henri provided one. He was happy to smuggle me out of Occupied France by the Chenonceau route. He enabled me to escape and make my way to America. It became simple from there. Only Moreau knew where I was. My ever-faithful friend. He kept me informed about Catherine, announced my fatherhood to me, allowed me to send funds through him to support Catherine and the child."

He frowned at his middle-aged son. "No matter how I felt about my first-born child, or his mother, I could never leave them desperate, as my own father had done. That was unthinkable."

Beaumont stared at his father.

I picked up the thread of the story, hoping to distract the pair of them. "But the note hadn't been destroyed."

"Which is precisely why we are here today." Fisher raised his gun as a reminder. "Moreau's call to me when he decoded the note was a shock. I couldn't believe it had surfaced after all these years. I wondered how he had managed to decode it. How could he have succeeded in identifying me? The answer to that, Ms. Lynch, came through you."

"What do you mean?"

"The copy of the note, in your fax to Nancy. As soon as I saw it, I realized what had happened. In my haste to escape, I made the unfortunate mistake of using a code already broken by the Résistance. This is what enabled Moreau to learn the truth so quickly, and precipitated his death."

"And the deaths of Toussaint, Marie and Claude."

Fisher hissed. "Do not neglect to add yourself to that list. The fact that we are having this pleasant conversation does not mean I have changed my plans for you."

"There is one thing I still don't understand."

"What might that be?"

"Once Moreau was dead, why was it so important to destroy all copies of the note? Wasn't he the only one who could decode it, and who knew your identity?"

Beaumont's eyes widened as he listened to this.

"Perhaps," Fisher said. "But I could take no chances. They are still out there. Still looking."

"Who?" I asked.

"The Jews. The Nazi hunters. They never forget. They found Eichmann, Barbie, Touvier, all of them. And they continue to search. Somehow, some day, somebody would have put it all together, would have found the note and eventually found me. The risk was too great. And the price for my safety was small. The lives of a few insignificant people. What did it matter?"

What kind of person could rationalize murder so easily? The man was insane, and dangerous. And I was not the only one who realized this.

Beaumont stared at his father, eyes wide and angry. "Do you consider my mother and me to be insignificant as well?"

Fisher sneered at him, unblinking, then turned to me. "Behold my illustrious offspring. I should be quite proud of him, don't you think? He's a minor thug, often in trouble, arrested many times. It isn't bad enough he is a criminal. He isn't even a clever one."

A smirk appeared on Beaumont's face. "You don't know, do you? About *Maman.* Here you are, ranting about the Jews. You never knew she was Jewish, did you?"

Fisher stared at his son. "What are you saying? Catherine was not Jewish. She was French."

"Her name was French. Her mother had married a Frenchman. *Maman* was raised as a Christian, but her blood was Jewish through and through. She hid this from you in order to protect you. She loved you. And you loved her. I know you did. And when you betrayed the Jews trying to escape, you betrayed *Maman* as well. You are a fraud and a murderer."

His outburst ended, Beaumont raised his gun.

I heard a loud pop, like a firecracker exploding in my ears. The air filled with acrid smoke. A noxious stench surrounded me—sulphur and copper—gunshot and blood. I closed my eyes and held my breath, waiting for the smoke to clear.

Opening my eyes a moment later, I saw Fisher slumped backward in the chair, eyes wide, a gaping hole in his chest. A bloody mess was everywhere, on what remained of Fisher, on the chair and the coffee table, all over Beaumont's clothing. I looked down. My sneakers and ankles were blood-soaked as well.

I fought the urge to gag. If I were silent, perhaps Beaumont would forget I was there, at least until he was calmer.

He didn't calm down. He broke down. Letting the gun fall from his hand onto the smashed coffee table, he sank to his knees on the glass-covered floor. "Papa," he cried as he held his father's head in his hands. "Papa."

He was sobbing now, long, loud cries. He attempted to speak to his father's lifeless body. His words were unintelligible. He knelt there and wept.

Frozen in my chair, I watched the scene for what seemed like forever while waiting for my heartbeat to slow and my breathing to return to normal. Then I rose and inched my way toward the door. I looked back once. Beaumont hadn't noticed me. I slipped out the door.

Once in the hallway, my adrenaline kicked in. I ran down the spiral staircase, dashed past the concierge and escaped into the street.

I didn't get far. I had barely made it to the sidewalk when a car pulled up. Three men got out and blocked my way. Oh shit! What now? Then I saw who it was standing there in front of me. Stopping short, gasping for breath, I collapsed into the arms of Inspector Béchard.

# Chapter 39

"What I still can't figure out is how you managed to find me," I said to Béchard, slurring my words ever so slightly as we sat on the terrace of a café in the Place de la Sorbonne.

Two days after my near-death experience, I was finally beginning to calm down. I was on my second scotch. Béchard said it would help me relax. He was right. It felt good to unwind and not be afraid. Instead, I was beginning to feel a delightful sense of accomplishment, not to mention relief.

"That is simple," he said. "When you were not in the *Hameau* as expected, I became quite concerned. I put out an urgent alert on you."

"An alert?"

"*Mais oui.* A notice to all officers in both Versailles and Paris. A detailed description of you and your last known whereabouts."

"You mean an APB?"

"*Qu'est-ce que c'est* / What is that?"

"All points bulletin."

He mulled this over, then smiled. "*Ah, oui. Exactement.* / That is it exactly. This alert included what you were wearing. That proved to be very helpful."

“How did you know what I was wearing?”

“From one of the officers who responded to your attack in the Métro. He is a big fan of Star Trek. He mentioned the shirt to me when he called to confirm that you had come to the Préfecture to report the incident, as he had instructed you to do. Which you had not. And one seldom sees a T-shirt from Star Fleet Academy on the streets of Paris.”

I laughed. “You found me because of my T-shirt?”

“*Oui*. A patrolman in the neighborhood where you were held saw you being escorted into the apartment building. But at the time, he did not realize he saw you.”

“Huh? What does that mean?”

“*Eh bien*, his shift was at an end. He returned to the station, saw the alert and remembered having seen you.”

“How could he possibly remember me? It only took a few seconds for them to force me from the car into the building.”

“Do not forget that you were covered in mud from your fall into the ditch. While he only caught a glimpse of you, he definitely noticed that, as well as your Star Fleet Academy T-shirt. At the time, he thought you were merely another foolish American who had consumed too much wine and gone swimming in the Seine.”

“Is that how I appeared?”

“Indeed it is. He assumed your abductors were assisting you because you were drunk.”

“If only he had seen the alert earlier and recognized me on the street, it could have saved me an hour of terror.”

“True. It would have put my mind at ease as well. I was quite concerned about you.”

I sipped my scotch. “I’m very glad you showed up when you did. And that the patrolman remembered the address.”

“Perhaps. Or perhaps seeing you in a wet shirt was the best part of his day. Anyway, he did remember. That is what mattered.”

"And it may have saved my life. I will thank him in person."

Béchard favored me with a lovely view of his dimples. "Speaking of your mugging in the Métro, the responding officer also told me you acquitted yourself quite nicely, becoming free from your assailant and remaining calm. I am pleased you were not harmed."

"I was a bit shaken." Also both furious and frightened, but Béchard didn't need to know that. Better he should think of me as fearless and strong.

"I hear that you managed to escape by fencing with your attacker. And that he was unable to take anything from you. Congratulations."

"Thanks. My boyfriend Pete taught me some basic fencing maneuvers. It paid off."

He raised his eyebrows. "*Évidemment* / So it would seem."

"I have to admit I'm a little disappointed in my skills as an investigator."

"*Pourquoi* / Why? Was it not you who discovered the truth about both Beaumont and Pecheur?" He put down his beer glass and stared at me.

"True. But by the time I figured out Pecheur's true identity, it was too late to take any action. I was already in Tattoo's car on my way to Beaumont's apartment, and possibly to my death. In the end, I didn't find the bad guys. They found me."

Béchard shook his head. "Nevertheless, *mon amie*, it was you who insisted all along that the traitor was responsible for the murders, you who developed the theory of the missing link, you who realized the importance of Marie's last word. You made the connection between Pecheur and Fisher. You simply had not yet connected this Fisher to the president of your company. Contrary to what you say, I believe you are to be commended for the work you have done."

My cheeks became hot. The man was right. I had a lot to be proud of. I had fingered the murderer as the traitor. I had unmasked J. P. Fisher. And I hadn't been anybody's victim. All in all, I had acquitted myself quite nicely. It felt good to hear him say so. "Did you ever learn what happened to Renoud?"

"*Hélas, oui* / Sadly yes. His body was discovered in the woods at Versailles, not far from the *Hameau*. He had been shot."

I gasped. "That's horrible. And cruel and senseless. There was no need to kill such a harmless old man. A tragic end to a sad life." I raised my glass to toast Renoud.

"Do you find it somewhat odd," Béchard asked, "that the traitor proved to be a person you were acquainted with?"

"I think perhaps the Universe used me to correct a karmic injustice."

He gave me a quizzical look. "Karmic injustice?"

"It's a Buddhist belief that whatever you do comes back to you. As if the Universe has a self-correcting mechanism. It seems I was part of the plan to expose Pecheur's treachery and bring about his punishment."

He appeared to consider this, but said nothing.

"Was the infamous note ever found?" I asked.

"We conducted a thorough search of the ditch where you fell; the note was found, but the water and mud in the ditch left it unreadable."

"I don't suppose it matters anyway."

He raised an eyebrow. "Why is that?"

"With the exception of Beaumont, everybody to whom the darn thing mattered is dead." Except for me, of course, and happily so. "So what happens to Beaumont now? And to Tattoo and the man in the brown suit?"

"We are searching for the two accomplices, as well as the driver. I am confident we will locate them soon. As for Beaumont, he will be charged and tried for five murders, as well as for the attempted murder of *Mademoiselle* Amy Lynch. I have no doubt he will be either imprisoned or institutionalized for the rest of his life."

"Sounds good to me. Will I be required to testify at his trial?"

"That is quite possible." He fidgeted in his chair. "If that becomes the case, it would be my pleasure to spend some time with you enjoying the finer things Paris has to offer. In the meantime, will you be returning to the U.S. shortly?"

"Actually, no. I still have two weeks of vacation. And my room and board are paid for the entire time."

"How will you spend this time? Will you return to the dig?" He reached across the table and took my hand in his.

Oh dear. Things were about to become uncomfortable. Under different circumstances, I could envision a relationship with Béchard. I had given serious thought to the possibility before finally realizing how much I cared about Pete. He and I had a good thing going. I didn't want to mess it up.

I took a deep breath, let it out slowly. "I appreciate your allowing me to collaborate on your investigation. I have truly enjoyed the time we spent together." *Not to mention those adorable dimples.*

"But?"

"But I have a life in Boston and a boyfriend there. He is important to me."

Béchard eased his hand away.

"Pete is flying over tomorrow. We'll spend the next two weeks doing the tourist bit. It'll be fun to show him around Paris."

"*Ah, oui, bien sûr* / Of course." A trace of a frown fleeted across Béchard's face. "And after these two weeks, will you return to your job?"

"I don't know if I'll have a company to return to. Nancy tells me things are in total chaos at the office."

Béchard placed his empty glass on the table. "I almost forgot: I have a message for you. My superior at the Préfecture has instructed me to convey to you his thanks for your assistance on this most troubling case. His plan was to write you a note, but I asked him not to do so. You have had enough of notes for a while."

"You can say that again!"

Béchard gave me a tiny smile. "I wish you well, *mon amie*. It was a pleasure to work with you." He rose and headed slowly down the street.

I smiled and watched his lovely buns fade into the distance. "Farewell, my friend," I said once he was out of earshot. "Live long and prosper.

# About the Author

Like her heroine Amy Lynch, P.K. (Paula) Norton spent her career in the insurance industry. When she and her late husband Jack traveled throughout the U.S. and abroad, they entertained themselves by sitting in restaurants discussing interesting ways to kill people. As they plotted all manner of mysterious deaths and mayhem, the world of Amy Lynch was born. Paula's passions also become an integral part of her series—interests such as archeology (Paula has lived in Paris and once worked at the archaeological dig described in Dead Drop), spies (Paula was a card carrying member of The Association of Former Intelligence Officers), Paris, Key West and fencing. The Amy Lynch Investigation series currently in the works will consist of at least four books, perhaps more. It takes Amy to Key West, Paris, Cape Cod and beyond.

When she is not plotting and writing, Paula is, well, plotting and writing. She is a member of Sisters in Crime, the Cape Cod Writers' Association and the Rhode Island Authors Association.

Paula resides in Easton, MA.

Printed in the USA
CPSIA information can be obtained
at www.ICGtesting.com
LVHW011927031223
765565LV00051B/1967